The Promises We Made

The Promises We Made

ROHAN JAIN

Srishti
PUBLISHERS & DISTRIBUTORS

Srishti Publishers & Distributors
A unit of AJR Publishing LLP
212A, Peacock Lane
Shahpur Jat, New Delhi – 110 049
editorial@srishtipublishers.com

First published by
Srishti Publishers & Distributors in 2021

10 9 8 7 6 5 4 3 2 1

This is a work of fiction. The characters, places, organisations and events described in this book are either a work of the author's imagination or have been used fictitiously. Any resemblance to people, living or dead, places, events, communities or organizations is purely coincidental.

Printed and bound in India

To my mom, for kindling in me the passion for writing;
to my dad, for always being my pillar of strength;
and to my sister, for being my best companion
through thick and thin.

Acknowledgement

Writing this book has been a delightful experience, and I owe my gratitude to many people for making this dream a reality.

My mom, for inspiring me to write a book. Seeing her go through her writing journey ignited in me the passion for writing. I would like to thank her for providing her valuable inputs and guiding me throughout the process.

My dad, for being my pillar of strength whenever I had any doubts about going through with the book. I would like to thank him for supporting me and having faith in every decision I have taken so far.

My sister Neha, for being the first person to read the book draft. Her inputs heavily shaped my writing. I would like to thank her for being the best critic I could have ever asked for.

More than one lakh members of my Quora family, for instilling in me the confidence to embark on the journey of writing the book. Their constant love has helped me evolve as a writer over the years.

My dear friends from my internship days at EPFL, Switzerland, for being the inspiration behind many of the characters and events in the book. The idea for this book developed while travelling across Europe.

Acknowledgement

My teachers, mentors and friends from Sanskriti School, IITK, IIMA, London Business School and EBS Germany for playing a major role in shaping my personality.

The editors and the publishing team at Srishti, for believing in my book. I would like to thank them for guiding me throughout the publication process and for providing their expert advice on every aspect of the book.

1

11 December 2013

I was the happiest person on earth today. I couldn't believe my eyes, and read the email for the hundredth time. My hands were shaking so hard with excitement that I had to keep the laptop down on my bed.

"Congratulations! You have been accepted for a summer internship at Ecole Polytechnique Federale de Lausanne (EPFL), Switzerland..."

I had always dreamed of going abroad, but that was just a dream. Till now. Till this much-awaited email.

I was brought up in a middle class background. My father, a government officer, worked very hard to earn money and provided us a decent lifestyle. But we did not have enough to warrant leisure trips abroad.

Ever since I was born, I had been taught the importance of education. I was a hard worker, and had always scored good marks in my exams. I was a proper nerd, one of those guys whom the other classmates remembered only a week before exams. I was the teachers' favourite and almost an ideal student. I was the student who always sat in the front row and scored the highest marks.

I had also prepared hard for the exam called IIT-JEE that almost every Indian science student appears for. It is the exam that makes the life of every candidate hell for two years. There had been days when the struggle used to become too overwhelming and I would battle thoughts of quitting. I was 6'3" tall, had thick black hair, blue eyes and a handsome face – at least in the eyes of my mother. Inspired by travel bloggers, I would consider quitting studies to become a social media celebrity. However, I had a great circle of friends who would pump some sense into me whenever I would have such thoughts, and I would get back to studying hard for the next exam.

I had managed to clear IIT-JEE with a three digit rank and had enrolled into the Computer Science department of IIT Kanpur – the dream of every Indian parent. Yes, I had fulfilled the dreams of everyone around me – my parents, my relatives, my teachers, everyone.

My real dream, however, was to travel and see the world. I wanted to visit as many countries as I could, and make friends all over the world. Whenever I read a novel describing a foreign country, I longed to travel and experience new cultures. I was an avid reader, and the novels I read made me want to travel even more. Whenever I would read a novel describing the romantic city of Paris, I would want to visit the Eiffel Tower. Whenever I would read about a couple in some a novel holidaying in Spain, I would long to visit the colourful monuments of Barcelona.

My desire to travel got stronger when I heard about the foreign internship options available at IITs. I had good grades, and could clear the criteria for those internships.

As a result, as soon as I got the chance, I started exploring foreign internship options. I applied literally everywhere – US, Europe, Australia, Asia, Africa and anywhere I could think of.

I did not care about the field I wanted to pursue. I did not care about the university I wanted to intern in. Unlike my peers who were very particular about which university they applied to or which professor they interned with, I simply did not care. I just wanted to travel and see the world. It could be any country and any city. As long as I got to travel, I would be happy.

And then I received this acceptance email from EPFL, one of the leading technical universities in the world, and probably the best in Europe. Anybody in my position would have been absolutely thrilled by the reputation of the university. My batch-mates, in fact, were jealous of me because EPFL had been a target university for many of them.

I, however, had only one thought in my mind. 'I was going to spend my summer in Switzerland, the paradise on earth!' Switzerland was considered to be the most beautiful country in the world, and I had been longing to visit Switzerland ever since I saw Shahrukh and Kajol romancing in the Swiss valleys in the movie *Dilwale Dulhaniya Le Jayenge*.

Excited, I started reading more about Lausanne, the lively city in Switzerland where I was going to spend my summer. EPFL was located at the centre of Lausanne. Apart from EPFL, Lausanne had another major university – HEC. While EPFL was an engineering university, HEC was a university focusing on social sciences and arts. The presence of two internationally reputed universities meant that Lausanne was filled with students from all over the world. As a result, Lausanne was considered a very good place to meet people from all cultures. The presence of a young crowd ensured that the city was lively during the day and even livelier during the night.

The more I read about the city, the more excited I became. I could not wait to go! Not being able to concentrate on anything else, I decided to read some more about Lausanne so that I would be fully prepared when I finally reached the city.

While reading random articles about Lausanne, I stumbled across an article on TripAdvisor named, "The 10 best bars and clubs in Lausanne". As the name suggested, the article provided recommendations on the popular bars and pubs in the city. Towards the side margin of the article, there were advertisements from various pubs in Lausanne. I clicked on the topmost link, which directed me to the Facebook page of the pub in Lausanne named McCarthy's Irish Pub.

I started browsing through the pictures on the pub's Facebook page, when one particular image caught my attention. It was of a lovely girl dancing, with her blonde hair strewn across her face. She was laughing in a very carefree manner, as if she had no worries in life. Her red lipstick perfectly matched her red sleeveless dress. Her eyes had a tinge of blue. Her face was the most beautiful face I had ever seen. Her expression was radiant, and she looked really happy in the picture.

I read the tag on the photo – Sofia Rosier. I clicked on the tag to open her Facebook profile. I drew in a deep breath as soon as her profile picture popped up. I couldn't help but admire the picture. She was sitting in a garden, seemingly a university garden. Her hair was long, reaching till her waist.

She had left them open. It was a sunny day, and the sunlight reflected on her blonde hair. She was wearing a light golden coloured sweater that perfectly complimented her blonde hair. She was smiling. Gosh! Her smile was so divine.

She seemed perfect, just like an angel. Everything about her – ranging from her hair to her smile – seemed flawless. Unfortunately, the rest of her photos were hidden from public view, and could only be seen by her Facebook friends. I looked at her photo for a few more minutes before I got distracted by a phone call from my best friend, congratulating me on securing the internship. I switched off my laptop and spent the rest of the day celebrating with my friends.

As the days went by, I completely forgot about the blonde girl, and got busy. I was fully occupied during the next few weeks with the upcoming exams and visa documentation. After all, I was going to apply for a visa for the first time, and there were just too many things to take care of.

2

Four months later...

"Ladies and gentlemen, we have landed at Geneva. The temperature outside is eight degrees. The current time is 13 hour 46 minutes," the pilot announced on the speaker, as the plane gradually came to a halt.

I put on my heavy jacket, picked up my laptop bag from the overhead cabin and disembarked from the plane.

I was instantly hit by a gush of cold wind, so chilly that it felt like a tight slap on my face. It was much windier than I had anticipated. I had trouble keeping my eyes open. I pulled up the hood of my jacket to cover my ears, and took out my sunglasses. I had always wondered why people wore sunglasses in Europe even on days when there was no sunlight. Now I knew the reason. It became almost impossible to keep the eyes open in such a windy environment.

I looked around and was struck by the mesmerizing beauty. There were snow-capped mountains as far as my eyes could see. The air, though cold, was fresh. There was a unique kind of calmness around the place, even with people bustling out of the flight and chatting excitedly. The place was clean and surreal.

I passed through immigration and went to the baggage belt to pick up my bag. Then I started searching around for the ticket counter. I was supposed to take the train from Geneva to Morges.

Morges is a small town, not very far from Geneva. My internship was going to be in Lausanne, which is a larger and much more popular town. The housing in Lausanne was limited and extremely expensive, so I had decided to take up accommodation at Morges instead. It would take me only around twenty minutes by bus to reach Lausanne from Morges. I was used to commuting long distances, especially during my school days in Delhi, when my school used to be an hour away from my home. I could definitely live with travelling twenty minutes every morning to reach the university.

Based on the research I had done before leaving India, I knew that the trains departed from inside the Geneva airport itself. But I couldn't see a sign to the train ticket counter anywhere.

I found a burly looking officer sitting on a bench near a burger joint at the airport, and decided to seek his help. "Hi sir, I am new here. Could you please tell me where I can buy a train ticket to Morges?" I asked him.

The officer seemed to be half-asleep; even though his eyes were wide open. He grunted and directed me towards a counter in a disinterested manner.

I started moving towards the direction he had pointed, and finally found the ticket counters. There were separate counters for domestic and international trains.

I went to the counter for domestic trains. There seemed to be a waiting number. People were sitting around holding a small paper with a number typed on it. There was a display panel at the top, indicating the next number to be scheduled.

I looked around for a counter where I could get my waiting number, but couldn't spot any. A young couple sitting on the chairs in the waiting area noticed me looking around confused, and pointed me towards a machine. They also said something in a language which I assumed was French, though I did not understand a word. Lausanne was in the French part of Switzerland, so I needed to get used to hearing a lot of French here.

I went to the machine. There was the outline of a hand on the screen. As soon as I touched the screen, there was a beeping sound and a small slip containing my waiting number popped out from below.

'Everything here is so hi-tech and automated,' I wondered. I felt like an old man who had been introduced to a computer for the first time.

I took my slip and went back to the waiting area, smiling at the young couple who had helped me find the machine. My number was ninety-three and the current number on display was eighty-two. Well, not bad!

After about fifteen minutes, it was my turn. The guy sitting at the counter looked even younger than me. From his young and excited face, he seemed to be either a new recruit or an intern. Either way, he appeared to be too excited. He found it difficult to even sit calmly on the seat, and kept jumping excitedly.

"Lovely day, isn't it? That would be sixteen francs," the guy said cheerfully. "You'll have to switch trains at Geneva Gare. The ticket is valid for the whole day. And what a day it is!" The guy's excitement was so infectious that I couldn't help but laugh as I bought the ticket.

So I had to first board a train from Geneva Airport to Geneva Gare, and then wait for a train from Geneva Gare to Morges Gare. The railway stations were called "Gare" in Switzerland, I deduced.

I looked at the board which displayed the train schedule, and was surprised to find so much accuracy in the schedule. Among the twenty or so trains listed on the board at that particular moment, I could see only one train that was delayed. I couldn't believe my eyes when I saw the magnitude of the delay. 2 minutes! That's it! Wow! I had never thought being late by two minutes was actually considered being late.

I boarded the train to Geneva Gare. Used to the crowded trains in India, I was pleased to see so many empty seats in the train. It was just a five-minute journey from Geneva airport to Geneva Gare, and I spent the journey gazing at the scenic beauty outside the window.

Geneva Gare looked like a very busy train station, with people rushing around. Compared to the Geneva airport, the station was much more crowded and noisy.

I searched around for the train to Morges and found the board which had the train details. There were trains every hour from Geneva to Morges. I boarded the next available train. This time, the journey took around half an hour.

I just could not keep my eyes off the scenery through the glass windows of the train. The landscape was mesmerizingly beautiful, with mountains, lakes and greenery, all blended to perfection.

As I got off at the Morges train station, I looked at my watch. It was 3:45 p.m. I had scheduled an appointment at 4 p.m. with the warden of FMEL Zenith, the student hostel where I was going to stay. I did a quick mental check to realize that I might be a few minutes late for my appointment.

'Being late by just a few minutes should be okay,' I thought. After all, no one in India ever reached any meeting on time. Well, I could not have been more wrong!

I had traced the path to FMEL Zenith online, before departing from India. FMEL Zenith was quite close to the Morges station – just a few minutes' walk upwards on a slightly hilly terrain. However, there was also an option of taking a bus from the station to the hostel.

"Once you get off at Morges Gare, take bus no. 702 to Zenith. Then ask someone for the way to FMEL," the warden, Christian Nydegger, had instructed me during our email interactions.

Fondation Maisons pour Etudiants Lausanne, or FMEL in short, were a chain of private hostels in many student cities of Switzerland. These were fully furnished hostels, and were only reserved for students.

While searching online for accommodation, I had come across many websites. While FMEL was slightly more expensive as compared to the other hostels, I had found that FMEL was the most convenient and trustworthy.

I had heard so many cases of fake websites stealing money from unaware students that I did not want to take risks. The FMEL hostels had excellent reviews, and were recommended by almost every student who had stayed there.

The FMEL in Morges was named Zenith and was one of the newer and smaller FMELs, having a capacity of only around thirty students. I had heard that some of the larger FMELs in the Lausanne city could fit as many as four hundred students.

I asked someone the way to the bus stop. There was a big chart at the bus stop mentioning the schedule of the various buses. There was one problem though. A problem I now realized I would face quite regularly. The days in the chart were mentioned in the French language.

"Excuse me," I asked someone, hoping he knew English, "Could you please tell me how to understand this graph? I don't know French."

"Yes of course!" The guy replied in a pleasant tone. "Today is Monday, which is *Lundi* in French. Here, you can see your bus schedule in the row for *Lundi.*"

It seemed like I would need to learn basic French very soon to get around this city. People, especially the younger generation, did speak a little bit of English, but all instructions were normally written in French.

The bus to Zenith arrived in a few minutes. I stepped inside the bus and went towards the driver to buy the ticket. As I had feared, he didn't know English. But on mentioning Zenith, he understood where I wanted to go.

I arrived at Zenith at 4:10 pm and looked around for FMEL. I didn't need to ask anyone, as the area had only one major building. It was a small building, standing out because of its brightly coloured paint. A mixture of fluorescent yellow, green, blue and red colours had been used to paint the building in the form of tiles. I assumed the bright colours denoted the young population in some way. There were a few bicycles parked inside a shed. I looked around to find the gate of the building and started walking towards it.

On my way inside to meet the warden, I saw a bald man coming out of the building. He was quite short, but had a muscular body and wore clothes that seemed two sizes short on him. When he saw me with my bags, he asked if I was Raj.

On seeing me nodding, he introduced himself as the warden, and reprimanded me for coming late. "Time is of the utmost essence here. It is considered very rude to make others wait for you without prior notice," he explained. "It's your first day here, so I am forgiving you. But I do hope you will not repeat this mistake," he added, speaking gravely.

I looked at the watch again. I was just ten minutes late. This did not deserve a scolding, especially when I had just arrived in the country.

I decided against protesting though, as it did not seem like a good idea to argue with the warden on my first day itself. 'What a welcome!' I thought as I rolled my eyes mentally.

Christian took me to his office, where I signed the contract and took the keys. His office looked as serious and sombre as Christian himself did – plain dark grey walls, empty except for a few files lying on the shelf. It was so different compared to the otherwise lively and colourful building. He then showed me around and told me about the rules and regulations of the place – No noise after midnight, no strangers allowed without prior notice and permission, no littering in the corridors, no smoking inside the room, and so on. It was a very long list, but he seemed to remember each and every rule by heart.

After listening to all the rules and completing the check-in formalities, I carried my luggage to my room. There were two floors in the apartment, and my room was on the second floor. There was an elevator, which was so big it could probably fit everyone in the building! I later found out it was designed that way so that people could easily carry their own furniture to the second floor, if needed. Some students apparently liked carrying their own furniture with them, as it made them feel more at home. I found that quite strange though, as I couldn't imagine carrying my furniture with me. I did not really have any special bonding with my furniture, and preferred travelling light. Cultural differences, I guessed.

The hostel had a common room and a kitchen, which were on the second floor. The washing machines were on the ground floor. Each floor had a separate bathroom.

My room was quite nice. Much nicer than I had imagined from the photos Christian had sent me. It had a large bed, a study table and a couple of chairs. I touched the mattress; it felt so soft and comfortable. I was really tired after the whole day of travelling, even though I had slept for a while in the plane. That plane ride seemed such a long time back now.

It was 5:30 p.m., which meant it was around 9 p.m. in India. My mom usually gets quite worried if she does not hear from me for long. This being my first time outside India, I was sure she would be feeling outright restless with worry. I had promised her that I would drop a message on Facebook as soon as I reached my room.

I opened Facebook and wrote a message to my mom that I had reached safely. I could not call her, as I did not have a local SIM card yet.

She replied almost instantly, as soon as I sent the message.

"How are you? How is your room? How is Switzerland? Did you eat something? Are the people friendly? Are you facing any problems?"

I laughed. I could imagine her sitting online the whole day, waiting for my message. I told her everything was fine and that I was tired and would talk to her in detail soon.

After that, I crawled under the warm blanket. I fell asleep as soon as my head touched the pillow.

3

"Oh fuck! I am so sorry!" I gasped hard, afraid that I had entered the women's bathroom by mistake.

Still exhausted from the long journey, I had woken up groggy on my first day at FMEL, and had decided to take a hot shower to refresh myself. I had just entered the bathroom, when I saw a sight that made all my grogginess vanish instantly.

A girl was standing near the wash basin, drying her hair. She was half naked, with just a towel covering her body. I apologized hastily and turned back to rush out of the bathroom, when I heard her calling me from behind.

"Hey! It's okay. These are co-ed bathrooms," the girl called out.

Co-ed bathrooms? What did that even mean? How could there be a single bathroom for both men and women?

I turned around slowly, unsure whether the girl was serious or was pulling my leg. The girl laughed on seeing my hesitation. Still laughing, she came close to me, patted my cheeks and said in a sweet tone, "Welcome to Switzerland, honey."

I did not know how to react. I was too shocked to say anything. Seeing me standing stupefied like a statue, the girl said, "You will soon get used to it. Now c'mon, do you want to take a shower or not? Or do you want me to help you take a shower?" she teased as she left the bathroom.

I stood rooted on the spot, and it took me a couple of seconds to regain my senses.

'What the hell just happened,' I thought as I entered the shower speechless, my mouth still wide open with surprise. Except in movies, this was the first time I had seen a woman almost naked. I was so shocked that it took a few seconds for my body to process what had just happened, turning me on a bit too late. I stood under the hot shower for a long time, trying to bring my senses back to normal. Thankfully, there was no girl outside when I exited the shower, and I ran back to my room.

Feeling normal after some time, I spent the rest of the day roaming around the town. Morges is a quiet little town on the outskirts of Lausanne. The residents of the town were mostly old people, which explained the quiet atmosphere. There was hardly any young crowd around. FMEL, the student hostel where I lived, was the only apartment that had students living in it. Otherwise, Morges looked like the ideal kind of destination to retire.

Leaving aside the sparse young population though, Morges was a very beautiful town. It was right on the shore of the magnificent Lake Geneva, which flowed through half of Switzerland. There was lush greenery all around, and people were very nice and friendly. The weather was also extremely pleasant. It was neither humid nor unbearably cold, making it just perfect to roam around the town. All I needed to wear was a warm sweatshirt, and I was good to go.

The houses were small and simple, like the huts that I used to draw as a kid. The roofs were slanting because of the frequent rains in the area. FMEL was just a couple of minutes' walk from the lake, so I spent a lot of time near the lake that day, gazing at the fascinating view.

On the other side of the lake, I could see another very beautiful city. On asking a few locals about that city, I found out that it was Evian, the city in France from where the famous water company "Evian" had originated.

Somehow, knowing that I could reach France by just crossing the lake made me feel quite excited, even though I knew it was extremely dangerous and probably illegal to swim in the lake. I was not that good a swimmer anyway.

Considering that I was living alone now, I had to take care of all types of shopping by myself. On asking around, I found out that there were a couple of supermarkets in Morges where I could buy some grocery. The best and cheapest ones were Coop and Migros, which were Switzerland's largest and most popular supermarket chains. Both of them were huge supermarkets where one could buy anything, from food to clothes. I decided to make a list of what all I needed to buy and visit one of the supermarkets the next day.

There was also a small museum in Morges, which resembled a castle. The museum had closed down for the day, but I took a few pictures outside the museum anyway. There were a couple of ancient tanks outside the museum. Apparently, they were real tanks that had been used during the Second World War. The tanks had been non-commissioned and secured by the museum for display now.

I spent the rest of the evening simply taking a stroll by the lake. I could see many ducks around at this point of the day. I noticed a group of tiny ducklings following an older duck, presumably their mother. The ducklings were moving in a straight line, as if they had been trained to do so. I gazed at the mesmerizing sight for some time. There was so much discipline in nature, and so much to learn from the natural behaviour of animals. If only people took out time to observe and reflect!

I sat near the lake for a very long time, lost in my thoughts, soaking in all the peace and happiness around me. It had just been a day since I had arrived at Switzerland, but I already felt at home here. The tranquil surroundings ignited a strange sense of confidence inside me. As I looked at the sun setting down over the lake, I finally felt ready – ready to embrace Switzerland in its entirety.

4

I had blended in so well at FMEL that it was difficult to guess I had arrived here just a few days back. I was now already on friendly terms with all the residents.

There was a small ground outside the building where everyone occasionally gathered in the evening to play football or volleyball. Considering that I did not know much about football, compared to the regular players at FMEL, I always chose to become the goalkeeper. It seemed to be the easiest and the safest role, though fairly important. For some reason, I was good at goalkeeping. In fact, I performed so well as a goalkeeper that I soon became known at FMEL as "The goalkeeper Raj".

I had also started experimenting with cooking. I did not need to cook as my mom had packed enough ready-to-eat meal packets that could feed the entire hostel for a month. In fact, most of my luggage consisted of just food items. Nevertheless, I still wanted to try my hands at learning something new, and cooking was definitely a very useful skill to learn.

I realized soon enough though, that cooking was not an easy task. I tried making a few *rotis*, but they were completely burnt. It was slightly easier to make gravy and *paneer*. I looked up for the recipe of *kadhai paneer* online and tried my hands at it. However, I was not sure if I had the time and energy to make paneer every day. Cooking was a very tiring chore, I realized.

Everyone at FMEL was very curious about Indian food, as they had heard many stories about Indian spices. I shared with them some of the stuff that I cooked, and they loved it. Especially the paneer curry, whenever I garnered the motivation to prepare it.

It was fun to watch how their eyes started watering even with a pinch of spices. However, they loved the food so much that they did not mind the tears. 'They would soon start finding their native food boring and bland,' I proudly thought to myself.

My mom had also packed some *gujias*, which I shared with the other students. They all loved the Indian sweet, as they called it. I was not such a huge fan of gujias, so I let them eat most of them. I would not have been able to finish all the gujias by myself anyway.

The night before I had to finally report at EPFL, I met Jan, one of the residents, in the kitchen. Jan was a German student, about to finish his exchange semester at EPFL. I was excited as well as nervous to start my internship. The nervousness probably showed on my face, because Jan asked me if I was alright. When I told him I had to go to EPFL the next day to start my internship, he asked if I knew the way to the university. I realized I didn't.

Luckily, Jan had a class the next morning at 9 a.m., the same time when I had to reach EPFL. Since I was new, he offered for us to go together in the bus so that I could know the way to EPFL for the future. That sounded perfect to me, as I did not want to get lost trying to find my way to the university, especially on my first day.

Since the bus stop was just a few minutes away from our place, Jan suggested that we could meet downstairs at 8:15 a.m. the next morning and leave together.

I tossed around in bed that night, sleepless with nervousness and excitement. I was actually looking forward to finally visit EPFL and meet my lab mates. I was also quite eager to know more about my project and the work that I was going to do for the next few weeks. All I knew about my project so far was that it would be related to Computer Architecture, and that my mentor would be a guy named Onur.

I had checked Onur's LinkedIn profile. Onur was from Turkey, and one of the senior Ph.D students in the university. He had sent me an email a few weeks ago with a research paper attached, asking me to go through it to prepare myself for the internship.

While I was excited to start this new journey, I was also slightly apprehensive about how Onur and my other future lab mates would behave with me. 'Would they be welcoming? Would they be rude? Or would they be indifferent?'

"Well, there is no use fretting about this. I would get to know soon enough anyway!" I muttered to myself, just before finally falling asleep.

5

Excited, I woke up at 5 a.m. and took my time getting ready. I really loved the showers at FMEL. They were hot water showers, and I was not used to hot water showers at home. If it were up to me, I would have just spent most of my time under the shower, with the water refreshing my mind every single time.

With some time to spare, I opened my laptop and started going through the paper that Onur had sent me as pre-read material. I had gone through the paper multiple times already before coming to Switzerland, but I started going through it again, just in case. I had not got the chance to look at the paper after reaching Switzerland, and I did not want to create a bad impression on my first day at the university.

Computer Architecture was a completely new subject for me, and I was not sure how much I would be able to learn and apply in my internship in just two months. I had not done any major course on Computer Architecture in my undergraduate studies so far, and my knowledge was limited to the internet searches that I had made while preparing for the interview. I had got to know that the lab was planning on taking interns only for the Computer Architecture related projects, so I had projected this field as my primary area of interest during the internship interview. Now that I had been selected, the lab probably expected me to be an expert in this field. Honestly, I did not mind learning more about this field. Computer Architecture was one of the fastest growing areas in the domain of Computer Science, and would be useful for me from a future perspective as well.

It was 6:30 a.m. I had to reach my lab by 9 a.m. I was hungry, so I decided to have an early breakfast while reading the research paper. Suddenly, I saw Jan come out of his room.

"Good morning Jan," I greeted him excitedly while buttering my toast. Jan looked at me with his sleepy eyes.

"Huh! What time is it?" Jan asked, completely confused. He saw the wall clock and was somehow relieved to see it was still just 6:30 a.m. "Wow man! You gave me a scare. You sure are eager to start working, aren't you?" he exclaimed, surprised that I was already up and ready. Jan had woken up to pee, it seemed.

"Nah! Just don't want to be late on my first day," I said, munching my sandwich. Jan shrugged and went off to the bathroom. He came back a couple of minutes later. "I am going to sleep for another hour. Wake me up in case I oversleep," Jan mumbled in his sleepy tone, going back to his room.

Sure enough, I knocked at Jan's door as soon as it was 7:30 am. When I did not receive a response, I knocked again, louder this time. Jan opened the door, looking lost and sleepy. He looked at me, sighed, and went off to get ready.

We left at 8:15 a.m. to catch the bus from the Zenith bus stop. It arrived sharp at 8:20 a.m. I still found it strange to internalize the fact that even a delay of one minute was considered a cardinal sin in Switzerland. Everything had to occur with complete precision.

I really enjoyed the pleasant twenty-minute journey from Morges to EPFL. Many other students boarded the bus on the way, so the bus was almost filled with EPFL students. The view from the window of the bus was so breathtaking that I was fully immersed in it. I was glad to have bagged a window seat, as I simply could not take my eyes off the scenery.

The beautiful Lake Geneva and the Swiss Alps created a mesmerizing and blissful view. There were green fields as far as the eyes could see, with cows grazing every few metres. Even the cows here looked healthy and happy. Everything was clean and surreal. I could just stare at the view for hours and still not get bored.

I was afraid I would turn into a philosopher by the time I left Switzerland. Probably this is the reason why the saints went to the mountains to meditate. The tranquil atmosphere could calm down anyone's mind.

When we reached EPFL, Jan pointed me towards the direction of my lab. His class was in the opposite direction. "I need to hurry now. Good luck for your first day!" he shouted and ran towards his class.

I looked around. The campus was awe-inspiring. I had seen amazing Google images of EPFL, but now I realized they had not done even an iota of justice to the campus. A spectacular building surrounded by lakes and mountains, EPFL was a university campus right in the middle of heaven.

I followed the directions given by Jan and reached my lab. I had visited the website of the lab a couple of days back and gone through the profiles of everyone, so that it would be easier for me to connect their names and faces to the work that they do when I finally meet them. I believed in doing my homework and preparation diligently.

The door of the lab building was locked. Apparently, I needed an access key card to enter the lab. Considering it was my first day, I obviously did not have any key card with me. Helpless, I took out my phone and started going through my emails to see if there was anything mentioned about collecting an access key from somewhere at EPFL. I could not find anything.

Desperate, I started looking around, when thankfully a student passing by saw me struggling and came forward to help. He smiled at me, and opened the lab door through his own key card. I thanked him and went inside.

I had been told that the lab was on the second floor of the building. I went up the stairs to the second floor and saw the door to the lab. There was a huge board right above the door, mentioning the name of the lab – *The Computer Architecture Lab*.

I was half-afraid I would need to wait for someone to open the lab door as well, but thankfully, the door was already open. As soon as I went inside, I saw Stephanie. I recognized her immediately from the lab website. Stephanie was the lab secretary, the "mom" of everyone in the lab, as per the description on the lab website. She was the person to reach out to in case of any administrative issues related to the lab.

I had been in touch with Stephanie over the past few months via email. She had helped me immensely with my visa documents and in finding accommodation. In fact, I had been able to get such a good room at FMEL due to her efforts. She had been gracious enough to offer help in talking to the warden and getting a room booked for me on priority.

Stephanie looked taller and slimmer than what I had expected from her photo on the website. She had short brown hair and a pleasant face. “Stephanie? Hi, I’m Raj,” I greeted her.

“Hey Raj! So glad to finally meet you. I was expecting you. I hope you had a safe journey. And how is your lodging?” she said in a merry voice, rising up to shake my hands.

I liked her instantly. She had a trusting and friendly demeanour. I guessed her age to be around thirty-five. I had a feeling that everyone in the lab loved her.

“Yeah, thanks! I had a great journey. My room is really nice. Thanks for all the help in finding me such a good accommodation. And I really love the city, especially the mountains and the lake,” I said, excited.

Stephanie laughed on seeing my ecstatic expression. “Yes, this sure is a beautiful country,” she added in her merry tone.

“Come, let me show you around. As I am sure you know, Onur will be guiding you during your internship. He is a senior Ph.D student. He has not arrived yet, but he is expected to arrive soon,” Stephanie said. “Javier!” she suddenly called and waved to a tall blonde man passing by with a cup of coffee.

“Javier, let me introduce you to our new intern – Raj. He will be staying with us for two months. Raj, Javier is one of our smartest Ph.D. students,” Stephanie said, winking at Javier.

“Ah, you flatter me as always, Stephanie. Hello mate!” Javier greeted me warmly. I tried to recall Javier’s details from the website. He was from Spain, and currently in his second year of Ph.D at EPFL. He looked very young. He had long hair, tied back in a neat ponytail. He had a jovial face and a funny accent. "Come, I'll show you around! Want some coffee?"

"Sure! I'm a big-time coffee addict," I replied, delighted at the thought of some coffee. This was true. I actually was addicted to coffee, and drank at least 3-4 cups of coffee every day.

"Ah, me too! We will get along very well then. Let us see who is a bigger addict here!" Javier laughed.

He took me to the coffee machine and taught me how to operate it. "This is our lab's coffee machine, and you are very welcome to use it whenever you want to. Onur is in-charge of the machine, and he is very strict about some rules regarding the maintenance. I guess he would want to tell them to you himself," he chuckled, apparently amused at the thought of Onur explaining the rules to me. I wondered what that was all about, but I knew I would get to know soon enough anyway.

He poured out a coffee for me and then showed me around the lab. It was a really nice and cozy lab, with comfortable sofas and beanbags at every corner. It appeared like I had come to the lab quite early, because I did not see anyone else there.

My thoughts probably reflected on my face, because Javier said, "People normally come to the lab at around 10 a.m. Except Onur, though. He is the boss. He comes at around noon – and that too if he really wants to come early!" Javier laughed. "We all just try to ensure that we are here before Onur comes." He winked.

The way Javier was talking about Onur, he seemed somewhat like a dictator. I was becoming more and more apprehensive about my upcoming meeting with Onur.

I saw Stephanie walking towards us. "There you are, Raj! Take these," she said, handing me some documents. "These have your login password and other account details. You will need them to access the internet and log in to your computer. Come, let me show you where you will sit for the next two months."

She took me to a corner of the lab, where I saw two empty cubicles. "You are free to choose any of the cubicles you prefer," she said, pointing me towards the cubicles. I chose the one near the window, because of obvious reasons. "Smart choice," Stephanie said, smiling, as she entered my login details into the computer.

"So you're all settled now," she said in her merry tone, as my computer booted up. "Onur should be here in some time. Hamza is out of town and will come back tomorrow. I will set up your meeting with Hamza for tomorrow afternoon. You will receive a calendar invite on your email sometime today. I'll be around in case you need any help."

Hamza Naciri, a Lebanese by origin, was the director of the lab and one of the most renowned professors at EPFL. In fact, he was renowned all over the world in the field of Computer Architecture, and kept flying around to attend seminars and give guest lectures. As a result, he was always very busy and it was difficult to get time from him.

Hamza was the person who had interviewed me when I had applied for my internship at EPFL. It had been a Skype interview, and I remember how strict he seemed during the interview, though he was trying his best to be jovial.

With nothing else to do other than wait for Onur, I took out the research paper that I was reading earlier in the morning, and started reading it again. I wished I had taken up a couple of the Computer Architecture courses as my electives during my third year of B.Tech. If only I had known I would end up doing an internship later in this area. "Seems like I'll have to work my ass off to understand this field," I said and sighed.

"Hello there! You must be Raj," said a voice behind me. I looked back to find a tall balding man standing behind me. I recognized Onur from his picture on the lab website. I would not say he was fat, but he was not exactly slim either.

"Hi Onur! Yeah, I am Raj. It feels great to finally meet you," I stood up nervously and shook hands with Onur. He was wearing a T-shirt that read, "I am the boss."

'So humble,' I thought, sarcastically.

"I see you have read through the paper I had sent. Or at least tried to," Onur said, pointing towards the paper open on my computer screen. "That's good. We will talk about your project in a minute. First things first though, I see you have already operated the coffee machine, assuming that the empty cup of coffee on your table is yours. Has anyone told you about the lounge rules yet?"

Wow! So this was the great Onur. Now I could completely understand why everyone called him the boss. Not one question asked about how my journey went. No chit-chat. Onur was all business, with a no-nonsense tinge to his tone. I could not help contrasting him with the mild and gentle Stephanie, or the jovial and friendly Javier.

"Actually Javier had operated the machine for me. And no, I don't know the rules yet. He said you would be the one to tell me the rules." I mentioned, clarifying in case he had got angry that I had operated the machine without his permission.

"Ah, I see. Glad to hear Javier had operated the machine for you. I was getting worried, assuming you are not an expert in operating coffee machines. After all, this is your first internship, right?" Onur asked.

"Yes, this is my first internship. I have done research projects before during my undergraduate studies, but no proper internship," I explained.

"Yeah, I thought so. Okay, so let us get the rules sorted out first. Come, let us go to the lounge." Onur started walking towards the lounge before even completing his sentence, and I followed the dictator like an obedient soldier. First the long list of rules at FMEL, and now another list of rules at EPFL. People in Switzerland really loved making rules, it seemed.

We went straight to the coffee machine. Onur taught me how to operate it. Though Javier had already shown the same to me, I was not very confident about operating it yet. As a result, I did not mind learning how to operate the machine once again. Especially considering how possessive Onur was about the machine. Anyway, learning how to operate the machine was critical to getting good coffee every day.

Once Onur became sure that I had learned how to operate the coffee machine well, and that I would not damage the machine while operating it, he started mentioning the rules of the game.

"Do not forget to clean the drip tray after use," he said. "Wash the brew basket after use. Keep the wet brew basket on the tissue paper and not directly on the table..." the list was endless. I tried hard to remember as many rules as I could. I had never thought making a cup of coffee could be so complicated.

After what seemed like ages, when we were finally done with the coffee machine, Onur started explaining to me the other rules of the lounge. Sofas were to be used only for sitting, not for sleeping (*I mean, c'mon!*). The snacks kept on the tables next to the sofas were to be refilled whenever they got over. There should be no littering in the lounge. The lounge needed to be kept clean all the time. The dustbins needed to be emptied whenever they got full. And the rules went on and on.

Once Onur was done explaining the rules, we went back to my cubicle. Onur asked me briefly about my coding background and the courses I had done so far in my B.Tech. He questioned me about my interests and my confidence level in the subject. I swear, I was more tensed answering his questions than I had been in the actual interview that Hamza had taken.

Onur described what my project would entail, and gave a brief timeline, with specific deliverables. I noted everything down as meticulously as I could, as I did not want to incur Onur's wrath on missing anything. I basically had to automate all the processes followed by the lab using Python, a coding language. The project did not sound as complicated as I had initially thought it would be, but there was still a lot to learn and implement. I had not used Python so rigorously before, but I was confident I would pick it up.

"Drop me an email if you have any queries. My room is just around the corner," Onur said and finally left me on my own. I looked at my notes as Onur walked away, extremely apprehensive about the upcoming weeks.

6

After a few hours of trying to make sense of the research paper and figuring out how best to approach my project, I glanced at my watch. It was 1 p.m., which was safe to assume that this was lunch time. I was very hungry by then, and I really needed a break from the boring research paper.

I went outside, exploring the campus and looking for something to eat. Unlike some of the students who brought their lunch from home, I had neither the energy nor the inclination to prepare lunch in the morning before coming to the campus. Hence, I decided to find a place to eat.

The campus was very crowded at this point of the day, with all the students outside for lunch. I could see groups of students huddled at every corner, chatting and laughing. It was a very lively atmosphere, and I wished I had a friend circle like this to hang out with at EPFL.

I looked around for a restaurant. I found a nice-looking café-cum-restaurant right in the middle of the campus, and decided to go there. That place was full of students and professors, eating and laughing animatedly.

A whiteboard near the entry of the restaurant had the food items for the day written down. I had noticed this as a pattern in Switzerland – most of the restaurants had their menus placed outside the restaurant so that people could check the menu before entering the restaurant.

Most of the names in the menu looked strange to me, considering they were all written in French. I tried to decipher what they meant, but I could not understand a single word from the menu. I checked if the menu had any pictures of food items, but I wasn't that lucky. I tried to take a look around at the plates of the people eating in the restaurant, wondering what to eat.

"Need some help buddy?" I turned around to see a cheerful young guy in a wheelchair smiling at me. He appeared just a few years older than me and was extremely thin. He had short brown hair and a smiling face.

"Yes, please. I am new here, and am just wondering what to try. Can you suggest something nice?" I cheerfully asked.

"Yeah sure, I can see how lost you are!" he laughed. "Follow me. My name is Emanuelle, by the way. You can call me Manu. All my friends call me Manu. You'll find Manu easier to pronounce as well, I believe." He chuckled.

I instantly knew we would get along well. I introduced myself and followed him. He asked me whether I had any specific preferences, to which I said I was open to everything except seafood. I had never tried seafood, and the idea of eating crabs did not appeal so much to me.

Manu suggested me to try one of the French dishes, and I ordered the one he had recommended. The meal consisted of rice, potatoes and a tempting curry. It appeared quite appealing, especially to my hungry stomach, and I could not wait to try my hands on it.

We took our food with us and went outside the restaurant to eat. I was impressed by how Manu managed everything on his own, despite being on a wheelchair. He took me to a group of his friends sitting near a table, and introduced me to them. They all greeted me very warmly, making me feel welcome. It felt nice to meet so many friendly people on my first day itself.

Manu was originally from Paris – which probably explained why he had suggested me to try the French dish. I should have guessed that from his name itself – Emanuelle. He had already completed his Master's from EPFL and was currently pursuing his Ph.D in Neurology. That sounded completely opposite to my usual field of research. He had just started his Ph.D a couple of months back, and was still looking for a thesis topic. He mentioned that he was now having second thoughts about the Ph.D, primarily because he felt working in the industry would give him a much better learning experience. As a result, he was just biding his time at EPFL until he found a better opportunity.

I had absolutely no idea that EPFL had a lab for neurology as well, considering that EPFL was primarily an engineering institute. Manu clarified that the neurology lab at EPFL was actually the best lab in Europe, and thus received millions of dollars' worth of funding from all over the world.

Vasiliki, or Vasia as everyone called her, was from Greece. She was slim, short and had a really tall neck. She had also finished her Master's from EPFL, and was now working at a start-up in Lausanne that was funded by EPFL.

Eszter was from Hungary. She was currently in her second year of Master's in Biotechnology. She was really pretty, and had brown eyes. Her brown hair perfectly complimented her eyes, and her smile added to her beauty. She had a habit of hiccupping every few minutes in a childish manner while laughing. Considering that she was the youngest in the group (I did not count myself as a part of the group yet), she received a lot of pampering from everyone.

Edgar belonged to Switzerland, and was working in a consulting firm in Lausanne. He was tall and very athletic. I could guess that he was a gym freak, seeing how his abs almost bulged out from under his T-shirt. He had long blonde hair that he had tied behind in a ponytail. He had completed his Master's at EPFL and came to the university sometimes to eat with his friends. I was quite surprised that he came all the way over to EPFL simply for lunch. The commitment showed how much he really liked hanging out with the group. Looking at the bonding among the members, this group seemed very close and special. They called themselves "The Lunch Squad" because they met regularly for lunch.

On inquiring, I found out that Manu, Vasia and Edgar had been in the same class during their Master's, which probably explained why they were such good friends. Eszter had been added to the group later, but she had also become an integral part of the group now.

The French dish that I had ordered tasted amazing. I had been slightly sceptical about trying something so new, but it turned out to be delicious. Manu asked me if I had liked the dish, and seemed proud of himself when I told him I had loved it.

After lunch, we went to the same restaurant and ordered some coffee. I could have coffee for free in my lab, now that I knew how to operate the machine, but I was having such a great time talking to everyone that I wanted to avoid going back to the lab.

Manu asked me for my Gmail address and told me he would add me to their Google group where they planned their meetings, so that I could also be notified and join them if I was free. This sounded awesome. I was officially being offered an invitation to join 'The Lunch Squad'! And that too on my first day at EPFL!

We dispersed after coffee. I went back to the lab and decided to work for a few more hours. By this time, the remaining Ph.D students had also arrived in the lab. While they were all very friendly, they looked extremely serious and studious. I, on the other hand, found it tough to concentrate on work. Not that I was not studious. In fact, my friends back in India would probably have counted me among the most studious guys in the college. But this was not India, and that was what made all the difference.

After a couple of hours, I checked my emails. There was an email from Stephanie informing me about my meeting with Hamza the next morning at 11 a.m. It seemed like Hamza was coming back to the lab for a couple of days, before heading off to another seminar, this time in Malaysia.

This meeting with Hamza the next day would be a very important meeting. As the Director of the lab, Hamza took all the calls, even though Onur acted as if he was the boss of the lab.

It was important for me to get into the good books of Hamza as early as possible, to ensure a smooth internship experience. After all, first impressions matter. Even more so with Hamza, considering how busy he would always remain during my internship.

I knew I had to prepare for the meeting, by thinking through the broad timelines and objectives of my internship project, along with the key milestones. I was sure Hamza would be interested to know about my approach for the project, and I had to be prepared with a good answer. I decided to prepare later during the night, as I had enough work to finish on my plate already.

After going through the remaining emails and deleting a few spam ones, I found that Onur had sent me another research paper to internalize. "Please go through this paper today evening – it would give you more insights about the project. We can discuss tomorrow," the email read. As always, the first thing I did as soon as I opened the research paper was look at the number of pages: *112 fucking pages in one evening! Are you kidding me!*

I did hope that Onur was pulling my leg, though I knew deep inside that Onur was serious. He would probably ask me about the paper first thing the next morning.

With the day turning worse and the upcoming night seemingly turning longer, I decided to scan my inbox further to find that Manu had already added me to their Google group. 'That was fast,' I thought.

There was a message from Vasia in the group. She was going to the Satellite bar at 7 p.m. with one of her colleagues, and had asked if anyone else wanted to join.

Satellite, called 'Sat' in short, was a bar inside EPFL. I had read about the bar when I was doing my research about the facilities available at EPFL a few months back.

Not surprisingly, Sat was a very popular hangout place for the students. A bar inside the university – how cool was that! I could not even imagine having a bar inside any of the universities back in India.

I knew I had a lot of work for the night, but I thought I could still do with a beer. After all, it was my first day at EPFL, and I really had the right to enjoy! I could work until late night and still try to finish the work, if needed. Having made up my mind, I messaged Vasia that I would be there by 7 p.m.

I checked my watch. It was 4 p.m. I had a few more hours to go, so I decided to go through the new paper Onur had just sent. I knew I would not be able to finish it, but I could at least start reading the paper.

The paper was more boring than I had imagined. It was also much more difficult to understand. I had to read each line twice or thrice to understand the context. As a result, even after spending a couple of hours on the paper, I had barely understood anything.

It was 6 p.m. already, so I decided to take a break. Considering that I had a long night anyway, I deserved to have a break when I could. I decided to get a cup of coffee from the lounge. I operated the machine carefully, trying to ensure that I had followed all the rules laid down by Onur.

Satisfied that I had executed each rule perfectly, I went back to my desk.

I opened Facebook to check my messages. There was a message from my mom, "Raj, how are you? Have you eaten your food?"

I couldn't help but smile. She was such a typical mother. I had not had the chance to talk to her in the last couple of days, so I dropped her a message explaining I was alright, and that I had already started making friends at the university. And yes, I had eaten my food.

After sending the message, I started browsing through the feed. Suddenly I came across a random Facebook group which mentioned a trip to Bern, the capital of Switzerland, being conducted that weekend by the Erasmus Student Network of Lausanne.

I had heard about Erasmus. It was a European Student Exchange Program, which also conducted a lot of trips and fun events for the exchange students. I was not sure if this was a genuine trip link or just spam, so I scanned the Facebook group in depth to satisfy myself. The link seemed genuine. It sounded exciting to be able to visit a city with exchange students from other countries.

On reading more about the planned trip on the Facebook group, my heart sank. The deadline for signing up for the trip had already passed three days back. They had closed the registration link now.

Damn! This trip had sounded so much fun. It would have been an amazing chance to make new friends. Dejected, I wrapped up for the day and started walking towards Sat. I really needed a beer now. Or maybe two.

7

Considering that Sat was inside the university, I had imagined Sat to be a quiet place, much like a café. I was in for a huge shock. The place was anything but quiet. There were speakers everywhere with loud music playing. There was also a large television blaring at full volume.

From the cheers of the people gathered around, I could make out that it must be a football match playing on the television. People in Europe were crazy about football.

I could see half a dozen groups of students chatting and laughing their heart away. The atmosphere was jovial. It was a pleasant sight. Finally, the kind of exciting student life I had seen in movies.

"Hey Raj! We were waiting for you." I looked around and found Manu, Vasia and someone else (who I assumed to be Vasia's colleague) sitting on a sofa in the corner.

I introduced myself to the new guy, Samuelle. He hailed from Italy and was working with Vasia in the start-up. The first thing that struck me about Samuelle was his cheerful demeanour. He kept laughing all the time and had an infectious laugh. He also had a rare talent of cracking amazing sarcastic jokes at exactly the right moments, accompanied by such hilarious expressions that you simply could not stop yourself from laughing. He was quite short, and walked like Charlie Chaplin. His comical expressions made his jokes sound funnier than they actually were.

I went to the bar to get a beer for myself. I looked around and, as usual, all the names were in French. I just ordered the first beer on the list. I must have made the right choice, because it tasted really good. Beer was my favourite drink, and I could make out a good beer from a bad one quite easily.

I was slightly hungry, so I decided to order a pizza as well. Not wanting to experiment, I decided to order the classic Margherita. After all, you could never go wrong with Margherita, and I did not want any random unknown stuff on top of my pizza. When the pizza arrived, I searched around for ketchup. I found a bottle lying on the counter and picked it up to pour it over the pizza.

"What the fuck do you think you're doing?" someone shouted.

Startled, I looked around. It was Samuelle, staring at me as if I had gone mad. He seemed livid with anger. "Eating a pizza...?" I replied softly, wondering what I had done wrong. Angry Samuelle was so different from the comical Samuelle I had seen just a few minutes ago. The angry Samuelle was really scary.

"You never use ketchup on pizza! *Never!* It's simply not allowed. It is the greatest sin you can ever commit, man!" Samuelle told me in a grave tone. "Do you understand that? The greatest sin you can ever commit. And I am dead serious."

I first thought he was pulling my leg. "But I always have pizza with ketchup!" I protested.

"I don't believe this. No buddy, you won't eat pizza with ketchup here. Not while I am well and alive. Period," Samuelle said. His tone had a no-nonsense edge to it.

I looked around at Manu and Vasia for support. "You can eat pizza with pizza sauce, but never with ketchup. Apparently, that's an insult to all Italians. They really hate it when people from other countries play around with their cuisine," Manu told me, shrugging. Vasia nodded in agreement, her face sombre.

It seemed like I had touched a highly sensitive point, so I decided not to argue further. Pizza was an Italian invention. And they were very particular about how to eat one. Having spent all my life in India, I was obviously not aware of such customs. Considering how people everywhere in the world had localized the pizza according to their tastes, I could understand why the Italians were pissed off. It actually made sense, now that I thought about it.

I apologized to Samuelle. But the realization that even something as small as eating a pizza can have so many varied customs really put me in awe. There was so much still out there in the world to explore. There was so much to learn and so many experiences to gather.

I bought an extra beer for Samuelle as an apologetic gesture, just to be sure. Samuelle calmed down after some time and returned to his normal cheerful self. Probably to break the tension, he changed the subject, "So ESN is conducting another trip to Bern! Seems like its their default destination now. I wonder if the organizer's boyfriend lives in Bern. Only that can explain why they choose Bern every single time,"

Samuelle laughed. My heart skipped a beat on hearing about the trip to Bern.

"Oh Bern again? Maybe because very few people could be accommodated last time. They had chosen a wrong date for the trip last time, with the exams just around the corner," Vasia said thoughtfully. "I know quite a few of my classmates who wanted to visit Bern but were not able to go because of the exams."

"Bern?" I couldn't help jumping in. "I saw the notice for the trip on some Facebook page today. I really want to visit Bern, but the deadline has already passed," I said in a disappointed tone.

"Oh, don't worry so much about the deadline. You can still join if you want to. But I guess you'll have to pay the full amount of the trip, unless someone cancels at the last minute, which does happen quite often," Samuelle said.

"The full amount?" I was confused.

"Yes. You see, ESN really subsidizes all these trips for exchange students. The complete trip is being organized for 20 CHF, if I am not wrong, while the actual cost of the trip would be around 70 CHF if you try to go by yourself. I think you can still join if you are ready to pay the full amount of 70 CHF. You would then technically be going as an independent tourist, though you can still tag along with the group," Samuelle explained.

"Oh! Are you all going?" I enquired. I thought it would be much more fun if everyone was going. I didn't mind paying the full amount because I was planning to visit Bern sometime soon anyway. It would be better to visit with friends or other students than visit the place on my own.

Manu and Vasia said they had already gone last time, and had some work. But Samuelle mentioned that he was planning to go. And he was also planning to bring a few friends along. That sounded great.

Samuelle advised me to talk to the ESN trip organizer once before joining the trip, to ensure that there would not be any issues later on. I decided to look up their contacts from the Facebook page and call them first thing the next morning. "Alice is probably the organizer for this trip too. She is a really sweet girl, so you shouldn't face any issues. Let me know if you do, I will talk to her on your behalf. I know her from before. Plus, I think she likes me," Samuelle winked.

"Oh, really now, Samuelle? You think every girl likes you, don't you?" Vasia said, punching Samuelle in the arm. We all laughed. I could sense some chemistry between Vasia and Samuelle, but I let it be.

Cheered up at the possibility of being able to go for the trip, I ordered another beer. This time I ordered the second one on the list, which tasted even better. Or maybe that was because I was feeling happier now. One great thing about beer is, that it is perfectly suited for both happy and sad moments.

8

The next morning, I reached EPFL a bit early. Jan did not have classes that day so I came alone. I knew the route now anyway, and I needed to get used to travelling to EPFL all by myself.

It was going to be a heavy day. I had managed to somehow go through the paper sent by Onur last night after reaching home, even after all the beer from last night. However, I had not found the time to prepare much for my meeting with Hamza, and needed to spend some time with a clear head to prepare a strategy on how to impress him.

However, first things first. On reaching the lab, I immediately logged into my computer and searched for that ESN Facebook page that I had seen before. I wanted to check if the page had the contact details of the organizer of the Bern trip. I found the contact of the organizer, Alice. Alice, I assumed, was the girl that Samuelle had mentioned last night.

Coming out from the lab so that I could talk without being overheard, I called Alice. Since Samuelle had described Alice as a sweet and helpful girl, I was hoping she would not mind. And as a last resort, I could always mention that I was Samuelle's friend. Just on the rare possibility that Alice actually had a crush on him.

"Hello, Alice here," she said on the phone. She was speaking so softly that it was tough to hear the words.

"Hi Alice, I'm Raj. I am an intern at EPFL. I got your contact details from Samuelle. I have a query regarding the trip to Bern," I said. I decided to mention Samuelle's name anyway.

She said something but I couldn't properly comprehend what she was saying. Her voice was really low. Before I could ask her to repeat herself, the phone got disconnected. I called her again. The phone rang for quite some time before she picked it up again.

"Hi Raj. Sorry, I was in the library and couldn't talk, so I just came out. What were you saying?" Alice said. She had probably rushed outside the library to pick up my call, because she seemed out of breath. Saumelle was right, she did seem quite nice.

I explained the situation to Alice and asked her if I could join them for the trip to Bern. I told her how desperate I was to be a part of the trip. When I finished, there was a short pause. I crossed my fingers, my heartbeat racing now. Alice thought for some time and said it should not be a problem if I was willing to pay the full amount, as then technically I would be going as an individual passenger, though I could still be a part of the group. Relieved, I readily agreed.

However, Alice added that they were planning to conduct a tour of the Bern Parliament as well, and had limited tickets for the tour. I might have to miss that in case the tickets ran out. They had bought tickets for the group already, based on the number of students who had registered. And considering that the Parliament only conducted tours on request, it would be nearly impossible to get another ticket for the tour so late.

I said it was fine. I would simply roam around the city by myself during the time they spent inside the Parliament, and would join them again later. I was not very interested in monuments and museums anyway.

"Great then," Alice said. She mentioned that they would all assemble at the Lausanne train station at 5 a.m. the next day and then leave together for the journey. "Don't be late, Raj! Looking forward to seeing you tomorrow," she added cheerfully and ended the call.

Yes! I couldn't believe my luck. With the plan for the trip finally in place, I started moving towards the coffee machine with a wide smile on my face, when I suddenly came across Onur. My smile vanished as soon as I saw his stern look. "Hey Raj, did you go through the other paper I had sent you?" he enquired.

I told Onur I had glanced at the paper, but was still going through it in detail. We could discuss the paper briefly now if that worked for him or in detail sometime later.

"Great! Let us set up some time next week to go through the insights from that paper and relate that back to your project. Considering it is the weekend from tomorrow, you would have time to go through the paper in detail. Block some time on my calendar," Onur said, walking away with his coffee. I could bet that I saw a glimmer of a sadistic smile on his face as he walked away. Little did Onur know that I was going to be spending the weekend at Bern. I would hardly have any chance to go through the paper there.

Sigh! I went back to my desk, and immersed myself in work. I had to prepare for the meeting with Hamza. The meeting was planned in an hour's time. In addition, I also had to show some progress to Onur, or else he would show me his real Hitler self soon.

I prepared a pitch for Hamza, regarding how much I loved the field of Computer Architecture, and how passionate I was about research. I went through the pitch a few times inside my head, to ensure it did not sound fake or over-the-board. I also researched the names of a few stalwarts in the industry, just to be doubly sure in case Hamza decided to ask me about some of my favourite researchers.

As the clock struck 11 a.m., I got up and started moving towards Hamza's office. I passed Stephanie on the way, and she gave me an encouraging smile and a thumbs-up. I smiled back nervously, and knocked on the door to Hamza's cabin.

"Come in," chimed the voice from inside.

I took a deep breath, opened the door, and went inside the cabin. Hamza was reading *The New York Times*, sipping a cup of coffee. I had seen Hamza during my Skype interview, but he looked slightly different in person. He was tall. And by tall, I meant he seemed to be at least 6'3". He had thick black hair, and a sharply trimmed beard. He was wearing an EPFL sweatshirt and loose trousers.

"Ah! Glad to finally meet you, Raj. I was looking forward to our meeting. I hope your stay in Switzerland has been nice so far? I had instructed Stephanie to take care of all your needs." Hamza smiled at me as I sat down.

I immediately liked Hamza due to his warm demeanour. Despite his popularity, he seemed to be really down to earth. I had expected him to be wearing really sophisticated and formal clothes, but Hamza did not seem to care about all that.

I told him about my comfortable stay so far, and how much I loved the place. Satisfied, Hamza started asking me if I had started working on the project yet. I mentioned the papers I had read so far, and how I was planning to link the learning to my project.

The discussion with Hamza lasted for around half an hour, and I was awe-struck by the time I left the room. Hamza gave me a few very pointed bits of advice on how I could ace my project, and helped me develop a completely different and innovative approach to complete my project effectively. No wonder Hamza was known all over the world for his knowledge and expertise. He was not just sharp, but also had a very intuitive approach towards solving problems.

I knew I would rarely get the chance to meet Hamza during my time here, considering how busy Hamza always was, so I made the most of the opportunity. He wished me good luck for the project, and asked me to feel free to directly reach out to him in case of any worries.

I looked at the clock. It was lunch time. The lunch group was not meeting that day. Manu was eating with his lab mates. Vasia had gone to Geneva for a field trip related to her work and Edgar had decided to skip the get-together that day.

Considering I had to start progressing on the papers before Onur became mad, I decided to have a working lunch. I bought a cheese sandwich from the campus restaurant and brought it back with me to eat in the lab while working.

I stayed in the lab till late that night and tried to finish up as much work as I could. I read the paper that Onur had sent me in detail, and made some notes. I also did some research of my own on that topic and read up further online. I read up so much on the topic that by the time I decided to finally wind up for the day (or rather, wind up for the night), I could call myself a mini expert on the topic.

I drafted a detailed email summarizing my insights and collating my queries related to the paper. I refined and iterated over the draft for a few minutes, gave it a final look and sent it to Onur.

After such a tiring day at work, I finally went home exhausted and hit the bed. I was so tired that I fell asleep as soon as my head touched the pillow. Or probably even before, considering I didn't even remember when my head had touched the pillow. I had a sound sleep, dreaming about the different paradigms of Computer Architecture, the algorithms mingling with the rhythms of my sleep.

9

The next morning, I woke up at 4 a.m., excited for the day to start. I took a long hot shower to freshen myself up, and got ready. I did not know if the ESN team had planned a stopover for snacks or lunch at Bern, so I decided to prepare some food to carry with myself, just in case. I quickly boiled some rice, and prepared a ready-to-eat packet of bhindi to go along with it. I packed the bhindi rice along with some gujias in my bag, and left for the Lausanne station. On reaching the station, I went around looking for any familiar face.

I found Samuelle standing in a corner with a group of other students, laughing hard in his usual way. "Hey there!" he called out when he saw me.

I went over and introduced myself to the other students. In Switzerland, when people of opposite genders meet, they greet each other by kissing first on the left cheek, then on the right cheek and finally again on the left cheek. I quite liked that custom, understandably.

The group consisted of five Italians, including Samuelle. They seemed to be good friends and probably knew each other since a long time. One of the Italians, apart from Samuelle, was a guy. The rest of the group were all girls. Apart from

Samuelle, none of the others seemed to speak good English. They tried speaking in English when I was around to be polite, but had a lot of difficulty conveying anything.

I decided to look for Alice, to inform her that I had arrived. I asked them if anyone knew where Alice was. They pointed me towards the food store at a corner of the platform where Alice was buying snacks for the trip. I went to meet her and reminded her about our conversation.

"Oh yes! Nice to see you here, Raj. I was actually waiting for you. You are lucky. One of the students called in the morning and said he will not be able to join because he was feeling sick. Since we already bought the tickets, you don't need to pay the full fee now. You can use his ticket. I saved the spot for you," Alice said cheerfully, giving me the ticket. "Also, you can visit the Bern Parliament as well with us now."

Wow! That was quite some luck. I had not just saved a significant amount of money, but also bagged a free slot to visit the Bern Parliament! I thanked Alice profusely, paid her the discounted amount and went back to tell Samuelle the good news.

After a few minutes, Alice came and asked everyone to form a circle around her. I could see around thirty people in the group, mainly consisting of exchange students from different countries. I guessed I was the only intern in the group.

She gave us some general instructions on how to handle ourselves during the trip (don't be rude to other travellers, don't make noise in the train, etc.) and explained the travel plan.

We would take the train straight to Bern, where we would first visit the Parliament. Considering the queue expected at the entrance of the Parliament, it was expected to be around lunch hour by the time we would be done with the tour of the Parliament. We would then take a short lunch break and then visit some other monuments around the city, before finally returning to Lausanne.

This sounded really exciting to me. While listening to Alice speaking, I saw a brown purse lying unattended on the ground. I picked it up to search for any signs of the owner, and found a name written on a corner of the purse in cursive handwriting. *"Sofia,"* the name read. For some unknown reason, the name sounded familiar to me. But I could not recollect where I had heard this name before. I looked around, and asked Samuelle if he knew any girl named Sofia here.

Samuelle shook his head. But at the mention of the name, one of the girls in the group next to us turned around.

My heart started beating extremely fast. This had to be a dream. It had to be! This was too good to be real. I remembered now exactly why the name sounded familiar. The image of a lovely, blonde German girl dancing in a pub with her hair strewn all over her face flashed through my mind, followed by an image of the same girl sitting in a university garden, sunlight shining through her glorious blonde hair.

"Sofia Rosier," I whispered softly.

She was the most beautiful girl I had ever seen. She was very tall, almost touching six feet. The photos I had seen on the Facebook page months ago had not done justice to her beauty. She was a damsel in real life, an absolute angel. Her stunning face and perfect figure reminded me of the actress Scarlett Johansson.

Sofia was the kind of girl I could have only imagined in my dreams. 'Probably this was a dream. That was the only way to explain this magic. Would I suddenly wake up to find myself back in my room?' I thought to myself.

She saw her purse in my hand and came over, almost as if she was moving in slow motion. I watched each and every inch of her body move towards me, with the wind ruffling her blonde hair. She was just a few metres away from me, but it seemed like ages before she reached me.

As she came closer, the air was suddenly filled with a sweet strawberry fragrance. I closed my eyes and took in a deep breath, her fragrance completely overwhelming my senses. I could sense someone speaking, but my mind had lost the capability to make any sense of the words.

Samuelle shook me hard, and brought me back to my senses. I opened my eyes to see Sofia standing in front of me.

"Hey! Sorry, this is my purse. Thank you so much. It must have fallen from my shoulders. I did not notice when I lost it. The purse has my passport and important documents. I would have been in so much trouble without it. Thank you so much for finding it. I will owe you forever for this!"

I was speechless. I kept staring at her lovely face, my expressions completely blank. I sub-consciously handed the purse to her, but couldn't stop staring. Was I dreaming or was she actually real?

"Oh sorry, I didn't introduce myself. I am Sofia. I am an exchange student here from Germany," she said, coming forward to greet me in the standard Swiss way by kissing me on the cheek.

I was stunned. It all happened in slow motion, and I wished time could stop then and there. I closed my eyes, and her hair caressed my face as she moved forward to greet me. Her soft cheek brushed against my cheek. I inhaled, and my senses were overwhelmed once again by that sweet strawberry fragrance.

My heart was beating so fast that I was afraid she could hear it. I looked at her again. She had an angelic smile, the perfect smile with dimples on both cheeks.

"Hi...I'm Raj...from India...pleased to meet you," I somehow managed to mumble in a stammering voice. Before I could further make a fool of myself, the train thankfully arrived and Alice shouted for us to board the train.

10

I was sitting with Samuelle and his Italian friends in the train, but my mind was still stuck on Sofia and her warm smile. Her strawberry perfume still lingered over my cheeks. I placed my hand over the spot where her cheek had brushed against my cheek, and closed my eyes to visualize her kissing my cheek once again while greeting me. I couldn't see her around. Maybe she was sitting in some other compartment with her friends. But I knew I had to talk to her and I was hoping to do it in Bern.

Suddenly Alice came around. "Hey you guys! All good? Let me know if you guys have any problems," she said in her usual cheerful voice and went ahead to look at others.

It seemed like Alice really enjoyed the role of the ESN coordinator. It seemed quite a tough task to manage such a large trip, that too at discounted prices. Alice seemed to be really good at her role. Curious about the mechanism of such organizations, and as a means to kill time and distract myself from the thoughts of Sofia, I decided to ask Samuelle more about ESN. Over the one-hour journey to Bern, he explained to me how ESN worked.

Erasmus Student Network, or ESN in short, was a completely student-run body, with annual elections to choose a student head. The student head would then invite applications and hold interviews to choose his or her team for the semester. There were such ESN bodies in all major universities in Europe, all connected by a common spirit of helping the exchange students settle down and sharing cultural experiences.

Anyone could become a member of ESN by paying a fixed membership fee, renewable every three months. They held various trips and parties for its members every few days. The members would pay less for each trip or party, while the non-members needed to pay more for every event. This way, if the members regularly attended all the parties and events, they could finally end up saving more than the membership fee that they had paid up front.

Since the Erasmus Student Network bought many tickets at once and in advance, they were able to get extremely discounted prices. In addition, many organizations gave additional special discounts to ESN on associating with them for events. And ESN worked on a no-profit-no-loss basis, which meant that they poured back whatever profit they made into conducting more parties for the exchange students.

It all sounded really interesting to me. I wondered why I hadn't known about this before. The entire concept of student exchange is not very common in India, and as a result, there are hardly any such large scale organizations for the exchange students back home. While the universities in India that have exchange programs have an exchange council to help exchange students, there was no centralized organization working across the country for such students.

On reaching Bern, we disembarked from the train and assembled outside the station. Alice handed each one of us a map of the city and gave us our entry passes to the Bern Parliament. She winked at me while handing me the entry pass, knowing well how lucky I was to get this chance. We planned to spend around a couple of hours in the Parliament on a guided tour, and then have our lunch.

My eyes were searching for Sofia, and I saw her on the other side of the group. I wanted to talk to her but did not know what to say. I was afraid I would say something stupid and embarrass myself. I saw her busy chatting with her friends and decided to talk to her later.

On reaching the Parliament, we were asked to form a line for the security check. I took out my passport and entry pass and put everything else in my bag. Alice had told us that we could not take anything inside the Parliament with us other than our passport and entry pass. Everything else had to be submitted, even our mobile phones. This was meant to ensure that our visit to the Parliament was peaceful and meaningful, and also to ensure that there was no security threat to the Parliament in any manner.

We were asked to deposit our bags in the locker room. The locker required a deposit of one Swiss Franc for the key, which would be returned later when we were done with our tour.

I opened my wallet to take out a Swiss Franc when I heard the most beautiful voice in the world again. My heart started beating faster once again.

"Hey Raj, do you happen to have an extra coin? I don't have any change. I promise I will return the coin," Sofia asked, her angelic smile clouding my senses as usual.

Sofia remembers my name! I was stunned once again and kept staring at her beauty. She probably mistook my silence for hesitation. "You can trust me," she added, smiling. "I won't run away with your coin."

"Oh yes of course, I do have an extra coin," I replied without thinking, and gave her the coin I had just taken out from my wallet, without even checking if I actually had one for myself. She took the coin, smiled and thanked me, leaving me completely mesmerized.

Once she had gone, I started searching in my wallet for another coin, and could not find any. Damn! What was I supposed to do now!

Just as I was about to start panicking, I saw a hand emerge out of thin air with a coin. I looked up to find Samuelle smiling widely at me. "Here mate, take the coin."

I blushed, thanked him profusely, and took the coin. Samuelle shook his head, laughing as he went towards his locker. "Men will be men," I heard him chuckling to himself. I couldn't help smiling. Samuelle was a good friend.

Once inside the Parliament, we were greeted by a guide. He was tall, slightly aged and spoke perfect English in a typical Swiss accent. The guide took us through all the chambers of the Parliament and explained how the Swiss Government works. I had always been interested to know how the most efficient country in the world makes its laws, and the tour was the perfect opportunity to do so.

But that day, my mind was not in my control and I found it hard to concentrate on what the guide was saying. Sofia was walking just a few steps ahead of me, and I couldn't keep my eyes off her.

I did grasp some salient points though. Switzerland has a system of direct democracy, where most important laws required a referendum from all citizens. Also, any citizen had the power to challenge an existing law by gathering fifty thousand signatures within hundred days, after which a national vote would be called. It all looked pretty complicated to me, especially for such a small country. But that was probably why Switzerland was a very diplomatic and peaceful country, with hardly any riots.

After the tour, we all gathered outside the Parliament to click some pictures. The view outside the Parliament was very scenic, with the Aare River adding to the beauty. I took a few pictures with Samuelle and his friends, capturing the lovely background.

Alice instructed us to have our lunch and then roam around the city for some time if we wanted to. We would all meet again near the Parliament after two hours and then proceed for more sightseeing.

Samuelle and his friends had not brought anything to eat, and went to a nearby restaurant. I wanted to stay near the rest of the group in case I got a chance to talk to Sofia. And anyway, I had got my own lunch, so I did not want to splurge.

I sat on the ground and was about to open my bag to take out my lunch when, to my delight, Sofia came over. I could sense her arrival through her strawberry perfume, seconds before she was there.

"Hey Raj, here's your coin. Just so you don't think I ran away with it. Thanks again! You have been a saviour twice today," Sofia winked. "What are you having for lunch? This looks really sumptuous. Can I join you?" She called her friend over and sat down, without even waiting for me to reply. Not that I minded. Rather, I had to try hard to refrain myself from jumping up in excitement.

I couldn't believe my luck, I introduced myself to Sofia's friend, Laura.

Laura was an Italian, a brunette who looked super studious. She wore huge glasses and seemed like the kind of girl who was always engrossed in books. She was also an exchange student at EPFL, studying in the same class as Sofia.

I shared the gujiyas and bhindi rice with the two girls, and they both instantly liked the food.

Sofia had brought along some bread, cheese and muffins, while Laura had brought along some spaghetti (Italians always have spaghetti with them!) and salad. Combining everything, it was a nice and satisfying meal for the three of us.

We started chatting while eating and I was finally able to overcome my hesitation. I think Laura's presence helped ease out the tension and I could talk to Sofia without mumbling.

I noticed that Sofia was friendly and considerate. She ensured that I was involved in the conversation and didn't feel left out. Especially considering the fact that I had very less in common with either of the girls, except for the fact that all of us had an association with EPFL.

I also liked Laura, who seemed like a really nice and friendly girl. She didn't talk much, though. She was more of an introvert, I guessed.

I wondered if I should tell Sofia that I had stalked her Facebook profile and seen some of her pictures long before

I had even arrived to Switzerland. I decided against it, not knowing how she would react. I had just started getting to know her and did not want to ruin my budding friendship with her.

After the meal, some of the people in the group decided to take a nap. Sofia, Laura and I, however, decided to go for some sightseeing. We had around an hour to kill, and none of us felt particularly sleepy. I would have blindly chosen to roam around with Sofia over sleeping anyway.

We saw a bridge some distance away and started walking towards it. It was apparently one of the landscapes of Bern. It was quite a pretty sight, I had to admit. The bridge seemed huge!

"*Kirchenfeldbrücke*," Laura said.

"What?" I asked, having absolutely no clue what Laura just said. I thought she probably just mentioned something in Italian.

"The bridge is called *Kirchenfeldbrücke*," Laura explained. I was impressed.

It took more time for us to reach the bridge than we had anticipated, because Laura kept stopping in between to take pictures. She was apparently a photography freak and loved taking as many pictures as she could. Not that I was complaining. Laura looked so happy while taking pictures that we couldn't help but smile, and let her continue.

We passed a small shop selling postcards and souvenirs. Sofia and Laura wanted to buy some postcards, so we stopped there. Sofia told me that everyone in Europe was crazy about postcards, and it was sort of a tradition to send postcards to family and friends whenever someone travelled to a new place.

I never understood the use of postcards when we could use Facebook, text messages and emails to connect. Sofia and Laura didn't agree though. They said postcards were a way of conveying how much one missed the other person.

The effort in buying a postcard, writing a message and sending it from a far-away place showed that the person buying the postcard really cared about the other person and remembered him or her even while travelling. That feeling just couldn't be conveyed through a simple text message.

"I'll send you a postcard on your birthday next year - you'll understand then," Laura said, seeing I was still not very convinced.

I also decided to buy a couple of souvenirs for home. Knowing that Bern was famous for its bears, I bought one of the small wooden bears on display. In fact, Bern had got its name due to the presence of bears in the city, and there was a very popular tourist attraction in the form of a bear pit at Bern, where one could watch bears in their natural setting.

We were about to leave the shop when Sofia's phone buzzed. It was Alice. She picked it up.

"Hi Alice…Yeah, Laura and Raj are with me. We are near the bridge…Sure, we'll be right back", Sofia said. It seemed like the others were getting ready to leave.

Laura's face fell. "I really wanted to take a photo with the bridge," she cried.

I laughed. "Don't worry, Laura. I'm sure they will have a photo of the bridge somewhere on the internet. I'll find a good one and photoshop you in it," I winked. She punched me playfully.

We started back towards the meeting point where we had left the others. Laura kept clicking pictures all along the way. I was about to point out that she had taken the exact same pictures on our way to the bridge, but dropped the idea on seeing how happy she was.

"So how long have you been in Switzerland?" I asked Sofia. I knew that she had been here for at least four months, considering that I had seen her Facebook picture in the Lausanne pub four months back.

"A little more than five months, I believe. Wow! Time flies so fast! I absolutely love it here," she smiled. "What about you?"

"Oh, it's not even been a week for me yet. This is actually my first outing since I came to Lausanne," I replied.

"Oh nice! How do you like Switzerland? And where are you staying?" Sofia said.

"Ah yes, everything's perfect. I love Switzerland, especially the pleasant weather and the natural beauty. I stay at Morges, which is a few minutes away from Lausanne. I found a room through FMEL, and I like the other students living in my hostel. It's like a big family," I said.

"That's great! I live in an FMEL as well, though I live in the FMEL near EPFL. Laura lives in the same FMEL. I completely understand when you say the hostel is like a big family. I feel the same," Sofia said. "But do let me know in case you need any help. I would be more than happy to help in any way I can," Sofia continued, smiling.

I liked how much Sofia loved helping people. She really did! Well, that was quite an incredible trait to have, I thought. And it was a very rare one too.

"By the way, what exactly did you say you were doing your internship in? Something related to Architecture?" Sofia asked. 'She remembers! She was paying attention to me,' I thought, my heart dancing with joy.

"Computer Architecture," I clarified. "It is not the normal architecture you are thinking about. Much less interesting than that. I basically work with semiconductors and computer processors, and try to improve their efficiency," I explained. "Actually, I took up this internship just because I wanted to visit Europe, and this vacancy had popped up." I winked.

She laughed. "I hope your professor does not know that!"

"Oh no! On the contrary, he thinks it was my childhood dream to pursue Computer Architecture." I chuckled. I still remember how I had convinced Hamza during my interview, feigning so much interest in the area that Hamza probably believed I would like to pursue a Ph.D in the same subject later on.

We reached the meeting place soon. Everyone was assembled there. "There you are. We were waiting for you," Alice said, waving to us in her cheerful tone.

"We would take a tour of the ancient University of Bern," Alice announced. There were loud *boos* from the group. "Oh come on, it's not as boring as it sounds. It is one of the oldest universities in Europe. There is a lot of history involved with the university."

Seeing that no one was convinced, she added, "Afterwards, we will see some bears in Bern's famous bear pit, and also take a look at the best chocolate shop in the city." Now that seemed to cheer everyone up!

The university was not very far. We reached in less than fifteen minutes. Alice was right; it was quite a sight. The university was founded in 1834 and was one of the biggest in the continent.

The university had requested one of its students to volunteer as a guide for us. We spent around an hour roaming around the university. The young student, who had volunteered to be the guide, indulged in a lot of talking, mostly about the history of the university and its ideology. But everyone was exhausted and very few people were listening.

The university had a great architecture, and the guide spent some time talking about it. On hearing the word 'Architecture', Sofia punched me playfully. I should have probably chuckled, but I blushed instead. Thankfully, Sofia didn't notice.

Once we were done with the university tour, which took about an hour, we thanked the guide and walked towards the bear pit. The famous bear pit was a popular tourist destination, though it was generally very difficult to spot a bear in the pit. The bears usually liked hiding in their caves in peace.

We soon reached the place. There was a railing, from where we could see the valley below. We could also see the Aare river and a lot of trees. It was like a mini-forest, preserved in its natural state. But as expected, we could see no bears!

I looked around and saw a group of people crowded around a spot, trying to squint at something. One of them even had a pair of binoculars on. We went near the spot and looked down.

After searching closely for a few minutes, we finally found what the group was looking at. There were two bears, hidden behind a big bush. We could only see their legs and a small part of their back. It seemed like they were sleeping.

There were screams of excitement, and we followed the pointed fingers to find another bear. This bear was sleeping as well, though he was much more visible than the other two.

That was a disappointment. I had hoped to see the bears moving around and playing with each other. I looked around and saw that the others were disappointed too.

Except Laura though, who kept clicking pictures of the sleeping bears, and seemed super excited. I wondered if the bears were even visible in her pictures.

We waited for some more time, hoping that the bears would move, but they didn't.

"I wish we could stay for longer, but we really need to move now. We still have to visit the chocolate shop, and then we have a train to catch," Alice announced.

"Where is the chocolate shop?" Sofia asked Alice.

"Oh, we'll pass it on our way to the station. It has some of the best chocolates of all shapes and flavours. But mind you, they are quite expensive," Alice warned.

We started walking towards the station, and soon reached the shop in a few minutes. I was surprised on seeing the shop, and I could notice that the others around me were surprised too.

When I had heard "chocolate shop", I had imagined a small shop selling chocolates in boxes. But this was completely different!

It was not just a shop; it was more like a chocolate museum. There were chocolates of all shapes and sizes. There were also some chocolate statues. I could recognize a big statue of Emma Watson, and another statue of Cristiano Ronaldo. Some of the chocolate statues were even bigger in size than I was! And that was something, considering I was more than six feet tall.

"I wonder who eats so much chocolate!" Sofia exclaimed.

"I know! And it can't be used just for decoration either as it will melt in that case. I think they probably use it in parties," I guessed.

Meanwhile, Laura had already begun using her skills with the camera. She was taking selfies with all the chocolate statues.

There were also some regular-sized chocolates on display in the shop. I could see dozens of flavours, all looking extremely tempting. Sofia bought a few of the mint-flavoured chocolates. I bought a few rum chocolates. I was quite fond of rum chocolates, and was curious to see how these chocolates differed from the ones we got in India.

The rum chocolates that I had in India were just rum-flavoured, without actual rum in them. These ones, on the other hand, had actual rum in them, so I was sure they would taste much better.

It was getting late in the evening, so everyone wrapped up soon. And before we knew, we were in the train on our way back to Lausanne.

11

"So, what are you guys up to tonight? Any plans?" Sofia asked in the train.

"I have to work on my thesis. I haven't even thought about my thesis idea yet, and I need to submit the initial proposal next month," groaned Laura.

"Oh, you have to do a thesis during your exchange?" I enquired. I had thought exchange was just about doing a few random courses at the host university, while partying the rest of the time.

"Oh no, this is for my home university. Since this is my last semester, I need to write a thesis at my home university after this semester. But most people start some preliminary work much before, so that there is less stress later," explained Laura. "My worry, though, is that I haven't even decided the thesis topic yet!" she added, groaning again.

"Oh, I'm sure you'll find one. You still have a lot of time. Which field are you interested in?" I asked.

"I want to write on something related to music," Laura said.

"Music?" I asked, surprised. "Wow, that's quite a rare field. I never thought one could write a whole thesis on music."

"Laura is a musician. She is the best viola player in Europe!" Sofia pitched in.

Laura blushed. "Ah well, I play okay," she mumbled.

I didn't want to show my ignorance in music by mentioning that I had absolutely no clue what a viola was. "Oh, that's awesome!" I said. "It's always a good idea to write on something you are passionate about."

"Yeah, true. I am a big fan of Mozart, and I want to write on something related to him. I am thinking of going to Vienna sometime for inspiration," Laura said.

Sofia nodded. Having no idea about the connection between Mozart and Vienna, I couldn't help but ask this time.

"Oh! Mozart is considered as the most gifted musician of all time. He had spent a considerable portion of his life in Vienna, seeking inspiration and composing music. In fact, he gained most of his popularity in Vienna. As a result, Vienna is very closely associated with Mozart's success," Laura explained.

'Interesting,' I thought. I didn't know this about Vienna. Not that I was surprised, as I hardly knew anything about music or Mozart.

"Now back to my original question, before you guys start another conversation and take us off the track," Sofia interrupted. "Do you have any plans for tonight, Raj?" Laura and I laughed.

"Well, I have no plans. Ideally, I should be working on my internship project, but I am not in any mood to do that tonight. So I will probably just either sleep or go for a walk," I said. In fact, I was wondering if I would ever be able to do anything productive here. There was so much to do which was much more interesting than working.

"Some of my friends have arranged a bar-be-que near the lake tonight. I am planning to join them. You can come along if you wish to," Sofia offered.

I was actually very tired and in no mood for a bar-be-que. But how could I reject an opportunity to spend more time with Sofia?

"Sure! I would love to join you. I have never been to a bar-be-que before." This was true. I had never seen a bar-be-que. In fact, I had not even heard of a bar-be-que before coming here. However, bar-be-ques were quite popular in Europe. It was an elegant way of spending time with friends, other than going to a bar, of course.

"Oh, awesome then! You will definitely enjoy. Bar-be-ques are fun!" Sofia said.

'With you, anything would be fun,' I thought to myself.

We slept for the remaining part of the journey. After such a tiring day at Bern, and a bar-be-que coming up, I really needed all the rest I could get.

12

On reaching Lausanne, the group started dispersing. Everyone thanked Alice for organizing such a wonderful trip, and promised to meet again in the next ESN trip.

Sofia asked Laura again if she wanted to join her for the bar-be-que, hoping she might have changed her mind by then. But Laura replied that she really needed to work, even though she didn't want to.

We bid goodbye to Laura in the traditional Swiss way by kissing on the cheeks, and wished her good luck.

I left with Sofia and we started walking towards the lake. A cool breeze was blowing and it was a pleasant evening.

"The bar-be-que was supposed to have started 2 hours back. We might be late," Sofia said.

"Had we been in India, we would have been the first ones to reach even after being two hours late," I joked.

Sofia laughed. "Actually it is only in Switzerland that I've seen such adherence to time. A few minutes here and there does not matter in Germany."

"A few minutes? *Woah*! That does make a lot of difference," I said sarcastically, ducking sideways to avoid a playful punch from Sofia.

We soon reached the lake. "So where exactly is the bar-be-que?" I asked.

"I don't really know, to be honest. I was hoping to find a familiar face somewhere around here who could guide us. Wait, I'll call a friend. He might be somewhere around."

Sofia took out her phone and called her friend. She spoke in a different language, presumably German, and then hung up. She sounded dejected.

"It seems like we just missed them. The bar-be-que ended just a few minutes ago. Everyone has left now," she said.

That was a pity. It would have been nice to attend a bar-be-que for the first time. And I was looking forward to spending more time with Sofia.

"Wow! A few minutes can actually make a difference," I said, trying to bring a smile to Sofia's dejected face.

"So what should we do now? We can either wind up for tonight, or go to some bar for a few drinks," Sofia suggested.

"Or we can take a stroll by the lake, now that we are here anyway. It is quite a pleasant weather." I suggested casually, hoping she would say yes.

To my delight, she agreed. *Yes!* A walk by the lake in Switzerland, with one of the prettiest girls I had ever seen! I didn't know I had it in me. Back in my college, my friends would have been so proud and jealous of me.

"So, Raj, tell me more about yourself. All I know about you so far is that you are studying Computer Architecture," she said, winking.

I had always thought talking to a crush about my personal life would be difficult. To my surprise, I had never been so comfortable opening up to anyone else. Once I started talking, it was a long time before I finally stopped. I told her about my life so far, my goals, my ambitions. I told her about the competitive examination system in India, and how one had to study their whole life to get into such universities. I told her how I had spent my entire life studying, but now I wanted to explore the world.

I told her how excited I was to have got the chance to travel abroad. I was the first one in my family to ever visit Europe, forget getting the chance to actually do an internship here. I told her about my ambition to visit each and every country in the world. A very difficult task, I knew, but I really wanted to understand the culture of every country. I also told her I wanted to study abroad just for the sake of travelling.

Sofia listened closely to each and every word I said. The fact that she took a genuine interest in knowing more about me eliminated any bit of hesitation left in me.

"So you want to pursue a Master's later on, either in the US or Europe," she observed. "In computer science?" she asked.

"I'm not very sure about the subject, at least not yet. I like computer science, but I'm not sure if I want to pursue a career in this field. I just want to study abroad, and computer science is one of the options. I am quite interested in management, so I might try for a post-graduation in management as well. Though I guess I have better chances of getting selected for a good Master's in Computer Science compared to management, due to my engineering background," I said.

"Oh, and is it easy for you to change your field like this? From computer science to management?" Sofia asked. "It's quite unconventional in Germany, and relatively unheard of."

"Yeah, many of my friends have changed their field after their Bachelor's degree, so yes, it is quite common," I said.

I explained to Sofia how most students in India choose engineering if they don't really know what to do, and then switch over after they realize their interests better. She found this trend quite amusing.

"I was just wondering, wouldn't a Master's be extremely expensive for you though? Considering that you mentioned your family is from a middle class background," Sofia asked thoughtfully. She spoke in a sensitive yet concerned tone, which really made me like her even more.

"Yeah, I know it would be expensive, and that has been bothering me for a while. I am planning to try for a scholarship somewhere. There are many scholarship programs available for Indian students, especially for the ones from reputed colleges. I have a good academic score, so I think I should be able to secure a scholarship."

"Oh, that's great! I really hope you can get one. You seem like a bright student, and I would hate it if you are not able to achieve your dreams simply because of financial issues. I would recommend you not to take a loan, though. Some of my friends have taken a loan and it's extremely stressful. They keep worrying about the loan, until they get a job. As a result, they are neither able to enjoy nor focus on their college life," Sofia said.

"Yeah, I also don't want to take a loan. If things don't go as planned, I might work for a few years, save some money and then try for a Master's. That would also give me some work experience, which is valued by some of the universities in the States," I said.

We talked about my life, career goals and fears for some more time. It was strange that I found it so easy to pour out all my feelings. I had never been able to talk so freely with anyone before. It also gave me a chance to think more about my goals. I had never really thought about what I wanted to do in so much depth before. Sofia seemed experienced and took a genuine interest in helping me, so I could rely on her opinion.

There was something rather gentle and encouraging about the way Sofia talked and asked questions that made me forget any inhibitions.

"So, that was enough about me. I want to know more about you now," I said, once I felt I had told her everything there was to know about me. I really wanted to know more about this really interesting girl now.

She told me about herself. Her mother had died from cancer when Sofia had just been a child, and her father had remarried a year later. So she had been raised by her father and his second wife. She had three step-brothers from her father's second marriage, while she was the only child from her father's first marriage. Her whole family lived in Munich. Sofia, considering she had studied in Berlin, had spent the last few years of her life there and loved it much more than Munich.

I asked her if she was close to her step-brothers and her father's second wife.

"My step-brothers and my dad's wife are really good people, and I like them a lot. They are kind and gentle. One of the reasons my dad remarried was so that I could have a family, as per my mom's wish just before she took her last breath. I think they do treat me as a part of the family whenever I visit them, so it's nice," Sofia said.

I noticed how she said 'my dad's wife'. This sounded like a strange phrase to me, as I was hearing it for the first time. I did not really know anyone in India whose mom or dad had remarried. 'Dad's wife', to me, had always meant 'mom'. Until today.

"Do you miss your mom?" I asked gently.

Sofia was silent for some time, deep in her thoughts. Just when I thought I had made a mistake by asking her this question, she replied, "I don't really recall much about her, unfortunately. I wish I could remember more about my mom. I sometimes recall a few incidents when I see my childhood pictures with her, but those memories are also fading away now. I can only remember a gentle smile looking down at me, a reassuring smile that still gives me the confidence that I am not alone in this world...that she will always be with me..." Sofia sighed, and went silent again.

I had a sense she did not really want to talk much on this subject, and had probably kept these memories locked away in her heart, out of anyone's reach. I decided to change the topic and asked her more about her studies and her goals.

Sofia was currently doing her Bachelor's in Economics from the University of Berlin. At the age of twenty-one, she was among the youngest in her batch. She was in the final year, and wanted to join a film production course after graduating.

"Film production after Economics? And you were telling me changing streams was quite unheard of in Germany," I said, surprised.

"It is," Sofia laughed. "When I decided to pursue this field, almost everyone around me was shocked. Quite a few people tried to dissuade me as well, but I was adamant. My heart was set on pursuing film production," Sofia said.

Having never met anyone before who was interested in film production, I enquired more about it. I asked her about the exact role of a film producer, and the distribution of responsibilities between a film producer and director.

She said that it was the film producer who held the reins of the film and made the final decision. The film producer owned the film, and decided the cast and other members. The film director just executed the orders or wishes of the producer. The budget was also entirely controlled by the producer, who usually obtained it from external investors.

"But aren't producers generally very rich people?" I asked Sofia.

"Oh no, they become rich eventually if the films do well. They don't have to be rich from the very beginning, though having money does ease the journey a bit. They just need to know how to secure money for their films. Imagine if you want to start your own business – you would have to reach out to potential investors, right? So does someone who wants to produce a film."

That was quite a large deviation from my earlier perception of a film producer – a rich person, usually either a businessman or someone with film background, who just gave the money for the film, while the director did rest of the work. But maybe the system worked differently in Germany, compared to the system in India.

As our conversation trailed off, I looked at the view around us. I had been so absorbed in the conversation with Sofia that I had completely forgotten that we were sitting at a scenic location.

The sun was about to set. The entire evening sky was filled with varying shades of orange, growing darker with time. In Switzerland and many other parts of Europe, the sun set at around nine or ten in the evening during summers.

Sofia took out her phone to capture the beautiful sunset. She then asked me to join her and we clicked a few selfies together with the sunset in the background. The pictures did not do justice to the beautiful sunset, but I was not really focusing on the sunset anyway.

It was getting colder now. I was also feeling slightly hungry, and asked Sofia if she wanted to grab something to eat. Sofia still had some bread in her bag from the Bern trip. She took it out and we shared the bread. None of us wanted to leave the sunset to go and eat somewhere else.

We sat quietly near the lake, soaking in the beauty of the sun going down behind the magnificent Swiss Alps, surrounded by the calm Lake Geneva. The only sound around us was the soft sound of the waves washing over the shore.

It was getting late. I glanced sideways at Sofia. She was still looking at the view, deep in her thoughts.

I wondered what she was thinking, but decided not to disturb her thoughts. I became engrossed in my own thoughts about Sofia.

I had initially developed a crush on her because of her pretty face and angelic smile. But after talking to her and getting to know her better, I realized I was more attracted towards her.

Sofia was sweet, gentle and caring. She had absolutely no attitude. She was not just extremely friendly, but also a very easy person to talk to. I could talk to her so easily without any inhibitions.

I had not really felt like this about anyone before. Sure, I had had crushes before. But those had just been short term infatuations. This was the first time I was attracted to someone's nature. I wasn't attracted just to her beauty. I really wanted to talk to her, spend more time with her, and see her smile. I wanted to make her smile, and I felt I could go out of my way just to please her.

I glanced at her again, only to find her looking at me this time, smiling. I smiled back.

"Should we go? It's getting quite late now, and I can see you shivering with the cold," Sofia said.

I had not noticed that I was shivering. I agreed. We got up and started walking back towards the station.

I couldn't help but think, this was probably one of my most enjoyable days ever. I decided I would not let this end here and would try to meet Sofia again, soon. I really wanted to get to know her better. And more than that, I wanted to spend more time with her. I had initially thought this was just one of my short term infatuations. But for some reason, I had a strong feeling that this was going to be much more than that.

13

The next few days passed by with me trying to finish work given by Onur, though he was never satisfied with whatever I submitted. Whenever I emailed him a report, he would email it back to me with multiple red markings. I wondered if he was expecting too much from me, or if he was just naturally being an asshole.

The highlight of the day would always be the lunch break meetings with Manu, Vasia, Samuelle and others. We met almost every day for lunch, and I really looked forward to those meetings. They gave me a good break from the daily rigour, and a chance to bitch about work.

It was fun sharing stories of Indian food and traditions with the Lunch Squad. They tried everything I brought with me for lunch. The Lunch Squad really loved all Indian dishes, though most of them were from ready to eat packets.

The more they heard about India from me, the more astonished they would be at how less they knew about the country.

They found it quite tough to believe, for instance, that people from the same country could sometimes not even properly communicate with each other due to different local languages.

"We sometimes have different dialects in the same country, making it slightly difficult to understand the other person. But the dialects still belong to the same language, with just minor differences in some words or the accent. I can't believe you have so many completely different languages!" Manu said, when I mentioned that almost each state had its own language.

I had grown quite close to the group, especially to Manu and Vasia. This group acted like my family in Switzerland. I could bitch about Onur and all my boring work with them. I could complain about how Onur kept sending back my reports with red comments on them. Manu, being a Ph.D student himself, always found it amusing when I complained about other Ph.D students.

But for some reason, I had not mentioned anything about Sofia to them yet. I didn't know why. Maybe I just didn't want them to think that I was vulnerable. That I had just met a pretty girl, spent only a day with her, and already started having such strong feelings for her. Or maybe because I myself wasn't very sure about my feelings for Sofia yet.

When Manu and Vasia had asked me about how the Bern trip was, I had mentioned it was great, explaining all the site visits. I had also mentioned that I made a few new friends during the trip, just in case Samuelle happened to tell them that I had been busy with other friends during the trip. But I had not really emphasized about any of those friends to the group and neither had I mentioned anything about Sofia. Samuelle also did not mention anything about her, probably ruling it off as a temporary crush.

Around a week after the Bern trip, I received a text message from Laura, asking if I wanted to join her and some of her friends on a beach picnic that afternoon. Laura liked organizing picnics and small parties.

It sounded fun. I asked if I knew anyone else who would be coming. She mentioned a name which I had not heard of, before mentioning that Sofia would also join. I said yes immediately.

We were all supposed to get food and drinks for the picnic, which we could then share with everyone else. This was Laura's idea to ensure that while she was the one organizing the party, she did not have to do all the cooking for everyone. I went to the nearby supermarket and bought some stuffed bread and a few beer cans.

I had not brought along any beachwear with me from India, but I had a pair of synthetic shorts, which I thought would be enough. It was a beach, and not a swimming pool, after all!

We planned to meet at the metro station and go to the beach together. I reached the station just in time to find Laura and a guy waiting there.

I greeted Laura in the Swiss style. She introduced me to her friend, Bruno – a very short and extremely thin guy from Brazil. He was her classmate at EPFL. I was surprised on hearing this, because Bruno did not look any older than sixteen. He was probably one of those people who looked like a kid, even after growing up.

"Is Sofia coming?" I asked innocently, trying not to give Laura any hint about my eagerness.

"Yes, she is," Laura replied, looking at her watch. "She should be here any minute."

Sure enough, Sofia arrived in the next metro train. She was wearing an off-shoulder black T-shirt and a pair of white shorts. She looked radiant, as usual. She smiled when she saw us and rushed towards us.

As I kissed her on the cheeks, I couldn't help noticing her strong strawberry fragrance once again.

Ah, how much I had missed that fragrance!

We started off towards the beach, talking and laughing along the way. The beach was not very far away, and we reached in a few minutes.

Laura had brought along volleyball in case anyone wanted to play beach volley. I had never played volley in my life, but there was always a first time for everything. I was a pro at playing badminton, and used to play for my college team. I figured I could learn volleyball pretty fast as well.

Sofia volunteered to teach me the rules of the game. The game was played in teams of two people. The basic goal of the game was to send the ball over the net to the opponent's court and prevent the ball from falling on our own court. A team could touch the ball up to three times before sending the ball across. A team scored a point when the ball touched the ground at the opponent's side of the net. The team that scored twenty-one points first won the game. The rules seemed quite simple and I was sure I would catch up quickly.

Once Sofia was done explaining the rules, she suddenly took off her top and shorts. Even though she took it off within a couple of seconds, my mind processed it in slow motion – with her slowly removing her top in a seductive manner, her hair flying around, before slowly unbuttoning her shorts and removing them. She was wearing a red bikini underneath her clothes.

My jaw dropped. I hadn't thought she could look more gorgeous than she already did. The bikini perfectly complimented her figure. It was all I could do to control my wild imagination. Sofia saw the expression on my face and blushed. The blushing red cheeks perfectly complimented her red bikini.

The rest of us also changed into our beach clothes. For Bruno and me, it just involved removing our t-shirts.

We divided into teams for the game, with Sofia and me on one side, and Laura and Bruno on the other. Sofia was the best player among us. Since I didn't know how to play yet, we figured this would be the ideal combination. Not that I was complaining. Even if I had known how to play well, I would have probably pretended to not know the rules, so that I could team up with her.

The game started. We lost the first game with an embarrassingly low score, though Sofia guided me well along the way. I think the primary reason why we lost was because I couldn't help concentrate on the ball when Sofia was bent down in front of me with her butt facing me, like a professional volleyball player. I kicked myself mentally for letting my imagination run wild, and decided to concentrate on the game in the next set. I picked up very soon and we won the next two games by a huge margin. Sofia and I were a great team. We had a perfect coordination and we could foresee each other's moves. Both of us were quite tall, which gave us an advantage; we could smash the ball into the other court much more easily.

As soon as I hit the winning shot in the last game, Sofia hugged me tightly with delight and gave me a peck on the cheek.

I couldn't help smiling continuously like an idiot after that. I had a suspicious feeling that the hug lasted longer than it should have lasted, but let go of that thought as one of my imaginations.

It was evening by then and we were tired after all the playing. We decided to dive into the food that we had brought with us. Bruno had some urgent pending coursework, so he had to leave shortly after we were done playing.

Laura had also brought along a bar-be-que stand with her and some bacons which we heated on the stand. "Finally your first bar-be-que," Sofia winked at me.

I took out the beer cans and the stuffed bread. Laura had also brought some chips and chocolates. It seemed like she was the perfect organizer. Even though she had asked us to bring food along, she seemed to have brought more food than all of us combined. We shared everything among us and had quite a filling dinner.

We chatted for quite some time about how everything was going in our lives.

Laura had finally settled on something related to the rise and fall of Mozart as her thesis topic. She was about to complete her thesis proposal in a few days, post which she was planning to visit Vienna for further research. She asked Sofia and me if we would like to join her for her Vienna trip, though she had no idea when she would be going. I thought that was a wonderful idea, and told her I would love to join her if my schedule at that time permitted me to travel. Sofia agreed.

Sofia had faced a very busy week with presentations due in almost all her courses, so now she was glad to finally get some free time.

I asked Sofia how her presentations had gone, and she said they had gone very well. She mentioned she was doing well in all her courses, except one – mathematics. "Numbers have never been my strong side," Sofia confessed.

I offered to help her in mathematics, considering that mathematics was one of my strongest subjects. As someone who had cleared JEE, I was sure I could handle whatever maths Sofia was learning. 'That would also give me more time with Sofia,' I thought. Thankfully, she agreed she could use some help.

Sofia mentioned that she had a maths exam coming up next week, and wondered if I could teach her sometime in the next couple of days. We fixed up a time for the next evening itself.

"Yayy, thank you so much!" Sofia exclaimed in delight, giving me a tight hug. Damn, I loved those hugs.

We sat quietly for some time, sipping our beers before Sofia got up, and went near the water. She stepped slightly inside the water, playing with the waves. The evening sun shone brightly through her blonde hair.

I took out my phone and snapped a few pictures of her. Sofia turned around and saw me. She laughed and posed dramatically for a few pictures.

I looked at Laura, who had fallen asleep on the mat beside me. It seemed like all the volleyball and excitement had tired her. She looked so peaceful and content.

I couldn't help but smile at how lucky I was to find such amazing friends in a land far away from my home country; friends I knew would last forever.

14

I reached Sofia's place a few minutes before 6 p.m. and rang the bell. The entire day, I had thought of nothing but the upcoming evening with Sofia. So what if it was just to teach her mathematics. In my mind, it was still an evening alone with her!

Sofia opened the door, smiled and gave me her usual hug. Damn! Did she wear her strawberry perfume even at home?

"Thanks for coming on such a short notice. You have no idea how much this is going to help me. I should warn you, though. I really suck at maths," Sofia said.

"No worries. You will do great, believe me." I smiled.

"Do you want something to drink? Tea, coffee or juice?" Sofia asked.

"Coffee, thanks. I love coffee," I replied.

"Me too!" Sofia laughed.

Wasn't she just perfect!

I sat down on the sofa in the living room. She brought two cups of hot coffee and kept them on the table. She then went inside and brought a thick book.

I glanced at the book – *An introduction to Probability and Statistics*. It was one of my favourite topics.

She saw me studying the book and offered, "You still have the option to leave if you want to. Last chance, before we dive into this scary book," she said and smiled.

"No problem, challenge accepted!" I laughed. "So where do we begin from?"

We spent the next few hours deep inside permutations, sample sets and probability distributions. I tried my best to explain the concepts in as simple terms as I could. Sofia was a very smart girl, and understood everything in the first go itself. She clarified her queries at the right moment, and was a dedicated learner.

Once we had reached a saturation point, Sofia said she needed a break. We had more or less covered the entire syllabus for her exam anyway. I agreed. Four straight hours of probability had worn me out as well. I was also feeling a bit hungry.

"Do you have anything to eat?" I asked Sofia.

"I have some cookies, but nothing heavy. I was thinking we could order some pizza. I have some beers to go along with it. What say?" Sofia asked.

I was amused that she had beers in her room, but did not have anything to eat other than cookies. 'Typical German!' I thought.

We ordered a couple of pizzas and took out the beer cans. The pizzas arrived in less than twenty minutes.

I suggested that we watch a movie while eating the pizzas, and Sofia brought her laptop. She had a large collection of movies on her hard disk. She asked me if there was any particular genre I preferred watching.

"Romantic." I winked.

Sofia laughed. "That's my favourite as well. Wait, I know the perfect movie to watch."

Sofia searched on her hard disk and started playing one of the movies. I looked at the title – *Notting Hill*.

"Have you watched it?" Sofia asked.

I shook my head. I had heard good reviews about the movie, though.

We started watching the movie and Sofia brought a few more beer cans.

It was a nice and lovely movie, with some amazing songs. I sneaked a look at Sofia, who was sitting next to me, deeply engrossed in the movie. She looked back at me and smiled.

As the movie progressed, I also got engrossed in the plot. Halfway through the movie, I felt some weight on my left shoulder. Sofia had placed her head on my shoulder and was watching the movie with her eyes drooping. I felt the familiar adrenaline rush inside my body whenever Sofia came so close to me, and tried my best not to move much lest it awakened Sofia.

By the time the movie ended, Sofia had slept on my shoulder. She was sleeping peacefully, and looked so pretty that I wanted to just keep staring at her forever.

Gently, I lifted her head from my shoulders and placed it on the sofa. I brought a quilt from her bedroom and placed it on top of her. The temperatures were dropping, and I didn't want her to catch a cold.

I looked at her for a few more seconds. Then quietly, I tiptoed out of her flat and closed the door behind me, making as little noise as possible.

15

Over the next few days, I was focusing on getting some more work done for Onur, just to prevent him from getting mad. He had started noticing how less time I spent in the lab, and I didn't want him to create obstacles in my personal life.

Sofia was busy with her exams. She had texted me the day after I had gone to her place.

"Woah! I didn't realize when I had slept! So sorry, hope you didn't have to leave midway through the movie. You could have woken me up, you dumbo!" Sofia texted.

"Don't worry, I saw the whole movie before going. And you looked so cute while sleeping that I didn't want to wake you up," I wrote back.

"Awwwie! You are such a sweet friend. I never got the chance to thank you for your mathematics lessons, though. Thanks so much! How can I ever repay you?" Sofia said.

"Just score well in the exam. That would be good enough for me."

Sofia sent back a couple of hearts as the reply. She used hearts quite often in her messages, but I had a feeling the frequency of her hearts had increased in the past few days. Was she giving me a hint? I really needed to stop over-imagining things in my head.

Since Sofia was busy, I utilized the next few days efficiently to catch up on my work. I talked to the other Ph.D students in the lab, especially Javier, to gain more perspective on my work, and incorporated their comments in my presentations.

By the evening before Sofia's last exam, I had not just caught up with the previous remaining work, but had also done quite a bit of work in advance, so that I could pace down slightly once Sofia got free.

To my pleasant surprise, Onur had started giving positive feedback now. Or rather, he had stopped giving negative feedback. According to Javier, not getting any negative comment from Onur was the most positive comment that one could get, so I did not complain.

Satisfied with my progress in the internship, I decided to take a small break and started searching the internet for things to do in Lausanne. There had been a few more links for trips nearby at the ESN group last week, but I had decided to miss those and focus on the project instead, so that I could spend more time with Sofia later on.

I saw a particular link that caught my attention, though.

"*Salsa classes in Grand Dance Academy, Lausanne*," the link read. I clicked on the link to get further details.

I had heard about Salsa, one of the most popular Latin dance forms. It was a couple dance and apparently very popular in Europe. I read the details of the classes on the link. The classes were going to be held in the evening, every Tuesday and Thursday, for an hour each. One could join without a partner as well and they would try to pair everyone joining as singles. However, there was a 20% discount for students joining as couples.

I wondered if I should ask Sofia for the classes. It would be an amazing opportunity to spend more time with her and also learn something interesting. In addition, Salsa was quite an intimate dance, and I looked forward to dancing with Sofia. If she agreed, of course.

The next day, as soon as Sofia's last exam got over, I texted her asking how her exams went. She seemed quite happy with her performance, especially in the mathematics exam. She thanked me again for helping her out.

I told her about the Salsa classes, and asked if she would like to join me. She asked more details about the classes and thought for a few moments. I held my breath as she took her time to decide.

"Sure, why not? Sounds like fun! And would also give us the chance to learn something new," she finally said.

Phew! I was so excited to hear this that I had no idea what to say. Salsa classes with Sofia!

I registered us for the classes. The first class was supposed to happen after three days, and I couldn't wait for it. I started googling more about Salsa moves to learn the dance faster and impress Sofia. Having never really danced any kind of dance form before, I didn't want to make a fool of myself before her.

We met outside the dance academy on the day of the first class. Sofia was wearing a tight sleeveless top and gym pants. As usual, she looked ravishing. We greeted each other, and went in together. There were six couples and around ten singles. The academy had ensured that the singles had equal number of men and women so that they could all be paired up.

The dance instructor was a Spanish guy named Sergi. The good thing was that he preferred to speak in English compared to French. He was tall and athletic and his bald head shone bright in the light, as if he applied something on his head to make it that way. He probably waxed his head every now and then. I assumed he was in his early thirties.

The instructor also had a partner, who was a former student at the academy and usually came to help the instructor in his classes. She was a local Swiss girl named Lisa, and spoke broken English. She was pretty, with shining blonde hair. Lisa looked quite young, almost in her mid-twenties.

Sergi spoke for a few minutes about Salsa and its history. Salsa had originated in Cuba around two hundred years back. The dance form had undergone many changes over the years and developed dozens of variations. We were going to learn the form of Salsa dancing called the LA style, or the Los Angeles style. There were also other Salsa dance form variations like the Cuban Salsa, or the New York style. However, the LA style was generally the most popular globally.

We started with a light workout session, where Sergi made us stretch our muscles and prepare our body for the dance session with some simple jumping exercises.

After the warm up, Sergi and Lisa taught us the basic steps of Salsa. Salsa had a lot of focus on musicality and beats. We had to separate the beats from the lyrics, and dance solely to the beats. Initially, it was very difficult for me to identify the beats in the songs being played, and I had to resort to following Sergi to sync myself with the beats.

The beats of Salsa go as "1..2..3....5..6..7....", so there is a pause after the third and seventh beat. The fourth and eighth beats are covered in those pauses. The dance has to start from the first beat, and all the steps needed to happen in sync with the beats. My problem though, was that I was not able to isolate the first beat from all the other beats in the song, so I had no idea when to start the dance.

I was glad to see that I was not the only one struggling with the beats, as almost everyone in the room was facing the same issue. Sofia, however, seemed to be a natural at Salsa dancing, almost always getting it right.

After learning the basics, we were asked to pair up with our respective partners. I held Sofia's hand with one hand, and put my other hand on her waist. With Sergi and Lisa guiding us, we started dancing together to the beats of Salsa.

The dance form was so engaging that we lost track of time. We kept dancing in sync till the end of the class.

I had not imagined I would love Salsa so much. Frankly, I had decided to ask Sofia for the classes only to spend more time with her. But I had to admit, I now started looking forward to my Salsa classes. Not just to spend time with Sofia, but also to learn more and more of this amazing dance form.

In the next few classes, Sergi taught us more Salsa combinations and also introduced us to another Latin dance form known as Bachata. Bachata was also a couple dance, but much more intimate that Salsa. The couple had to almost hug each other the entire time while dancing. Just like Salsa, there were different variations of Bachata as well, but the form that we learned was called "Sensual Bachata".

While steps were important in Salsa, it was the chemistry between the couple that really mattered the most in Bachata. With the couple so close to each other, the viewers couldn't help but admire the couple's chemistry, with their gazes hardly ever focusing on the steps.

The couple had to dance with their bodies together, their faces touching each other. When I held Sofia so close, her strawberry fragrance filled my nose and senses. As a result, I had difficulty concentrating on learning the dance form. On top of that, with Sofia so close to me, I found it tough to control myself. My body, after all, had a mind of its own.

To make matters worse, Sergi generally dimmed the lights when we were practising Bachata. His idea was to create the ambience for a sensual dance and to ensure that we could dance without being conscious of our surroundings. I had to admire Sofia for how comfortable she felt dancing so close to me, and I slowly got used to the intimacy.

I started liking Bachata more than Salsa. Not just because I got to be closer to Sofia, but also because Bachata was slower and easier to learn. Primarily, though, I loved Bachata because I got to be closer to Sofia.

If only my parents back in India had any idea where their nerdy son was spending his time these days!

16

Laura, Sofia and I started making travel plans together to travel whenever we got the chance. Every weekend, we decided to visit at least one new loacation. We generally targeted locations in Switzerland itself, because a weekend was never enough to cover anything outside the country.

One of the weekends, we decided to go hiking. Switzerland is famous for its hiking trails, and every local loves hiking. We asked around and finally settled on Creux du Van based on reviews from the regular hikers. Creux du Van was neither a very hard hiking trail, nor a very easy one, which made it just right for people who wanted to experience real hiking for the first time. The trail was meant for people like me specifically, since Sofia and Laura were used to hiking and could also hike in difficult trails.

We woke up early to take a 4 a.m. train from Lausanne station to Neuchatel, from where we were supposed to start our hike to Creux du Van. Neuchatel, was known for the origin of the very dangerous alcoholic drink called Absinthe. I had not even heard of the drink before that day, but I was introduced to it in a way that I would never forget.

On our way to Neuchatel, there was a bearded saintly-looking man sitting opposite to us in the train. His hair was tied in a ponytail, and his beard was long enough to touch his chest. He had a very small cup in his hand, the mini sized cup that we usually use to take cough medicines. He had a bottle tied around his neck. He was pouring something from the bottle in that small cup and drinking it slowly.

Considering that it was so early in the morning, both Sofia and Laura were sleeping in the train. I was not feeling particularly sleepy, so I decided to observe the bearded stranger, who seemed really interesting to me. Not that I had any interest in bearded men. No, not at all. It was just that this guy had a distinct appearance. I noticed he was wearing earrings, and seemed to have piercings around his eyebrows too.

The man probably saw me staring, and asked if I wanted to try the drink. I asked him what the drink was, and he mentioned it was Absinthe. I had absolutely no idea what Absinthe was. Being adventurous, and probably assuming that Absinthe was a normal local drink, I decided to give it a try. After all, how bad could a few millilitres of any drink be?

He poured a sip in the small cup and gave it to me, asking me to be gentle with the drink. I held the cup and took the entire sip in one go, completely ignoring his advice to be gentle with the drink.

“Argghhh!!! What the fuck!” I shouted, my mind spinning in circles, an intense pain in my throat. It felt like hot acid, instantly hitting my brain.

My scream woke up Sofia and Laura, who asked what happened. I was too dazed to reply, my vision blurred. By then, they saw the bearded man giving me an amused look, with the drink in his hand. They saw the bottle in the man's hand, and the small cup in my hand, and put the pieces together. After that, they started laughing so crazily that they couldn't stop!

They mentioned that Absinthe had such strong alcohol content that it was sometimes considered a drug and was actually banned in many countries. My mind was still spinning too fast to process all that information.

As Sofia and Laura kept laughing, I started drifting into sleep. I think the sleep was my mind's safety mechanism to bring me back to life. I slept all the way to Neuchatel.

Sofia and Laura woke me up when we reached Neuchatel. I was still slightly dizzy, but much better than before. The two girls still had a grin on their face. "I can't believe you had Absinthe just before an early morning hike," Sofia taunted me, amusingly.

We started the hike from the base of the hill. There was a thin trail guiding us along. The first hour of the hike was quite easy, even for the drunken me, after which the slope started becoming steeper.

Sofia, being the fittest among the three of us, was leading the way. I had to put in all my energy and effort in the hike, just to match my pace with the two.

After around three hours of walking continuously, we decided to take a break and have something to eat. We had all bought some light food items from the Lausanne station in the morning – easy to carry items such as bread, cheese, apples and so on. We found a nice place to sit and stretched our legs. While the other two started on the food directly, I took a few more minutes relaxing my muscles before joining them in the eating.

We relaxed for around an hour, before resuming our hike. It was late afternoon by the time we reached the top. The view from the top was hidden while we were climbing, but instantly became visible as soon as we reached the top.

"Wowww!" The three of us exclaimed in unison.

The view was breath-taking, to say the least. We could see vast expanse of forests, rivers and snow-covered mountains all around us, intermingling with each other to create a heavenly view.

We stood transfixed for a few minutes, taking in the view. I closed my eyes, lifted my arms and took a deep breath. 'This is how life is supposed to be,' I thought and sighed happily.

From the corner of my eyes, I saw Sofia admiring the view quietly, deep in thoughts. She seemed to be at peace, completely lost in the view. She seemed so calm and gentle that I couldn't remove my gaze from her. She looked back at me and smiled. She gently came closer to me, and wrapped her hands around my arm, resting her head on my shoulder. Somehow, at that very moment, I knew I was going to be in deep trouble. I was falling in love. I didn't know what love really meant, but all I knew was that I would do anything in the world to make this girl happy.

The sun was about to set, and it was getting late. It grew colder, and a slight breeze started blowing. We put on our jackets, took one last long look at the view, and started our journey back down the hill.

For the return journey, we took a shorter path. Getting down was much easier than going up and required much less energy. As a result, we reached the base very quickly.

It had grown dark by the time we took the train back from Neuchatel to Lausanne. All three of us were quiet. We were all extremely exhausted, and had no energy left to chat.

Laura had fallen asleep. I stole a glance at Sofia. She was gazing out of the window, deep in her own thoughts. I wondered what was going on in her mind. Was she thinking about me as well?

I could sense a strange feeling inside me, a feeling that was really unknown. I just wanted to keep looking at Sofia. Deep inside, I knew I wanted to keep looking at her smile all the time. Always...

17

The Salsa and Bachata classes were going great. Sofia and I had learned the dance steps pretty well by now, and were easily the best in the class. Our dance instructor even mentioned that Sofia and I had the best chemistry when it came to dancing. I blushed whenever I heard that compliment, wondering if he could see through my feelings for Sofia.

The dance gave me a chance not just to meet Sofia regularly, but also to stay close to her. The more time I spent with her, the more my heart started pumping whenever I saw her.

I was just living in the moment, trying to spend as much time with Sofia as possible. I was scared to confess my feelings to Sofia, afraid to lose her even as a friend. I was in the classic self-imposed friend-zone faced by so many guys who were afraid to express their feelings.

One fine day, Laura invited the two of us to her house. It was her flatmate's birthday and Laura wanted to throw a party for her.

I had never met Laura's flatmate, so I had no idea what I should buy as a gift for her. Like Laura, her flatmate Pia was also an Italian. I finally decided to go with a bottle of Italian wine, as Italians love their local wines.

Laura had also invited some of Pia's friends. There were around fifteen people in the party. It was a small but nice gathering. I met a lot of familiar faces too as most of them were students at EPFL. I had seen some of them around on campus, but had not talked to most of them before.

Laura introduced me to Pia. I wished her a happy birthday and gave her the wine. Her face lit up on seeing the label. "You have a very good taste in wine," Pia winked.

Delighted that the gift was appreciated, I went around looking for Sofia. I found her chatting with some other guests. She was wearing a red sleeveless dress, and had kept her blonde hair open. As usual, she looked absolutely stunning.

I quietly went up behind her and placed my hands over her eyes. "Guess who?" I asked.

She smiled. "My Indian buddy," she said, removing my hands and giving me a hug. "Your Indian accent will always give you away." She laughed.

I introduced myself to the other guests. Since Pia was a full-time Bachelor's student at EPFL, most of the students were from her class.

As the party progressed, Laura, the host *(Laura loved being the host!)*, brought out food, whisky and wine. The Italian wine bottle I had brought was also opened. Someone turned on the music and we enjoyed the delicious food and the ambience.

Laura seemed abnormally excited, so I couldn't help but ask her if she was okay. She excitedly whispered in my ear, "There is going to be a big surprise for Pia. I am so excited! Just wait and watch."

I hated suspense, but Laura didn't share the surprise with me. She kept telling me to wait and watch. I asked Sofia, who was standing next to me, if she knew what the surprise was. She also had no idea. With no other option, I tried to keep my curiosity under control and enjoy the party.

After a few minutes, Laura suddenly stopped the music.

"Hey everyone! I know you want to continue dancing, but it is time for Pia's birthday speech! Wohooo!" she shouted excitedly.

Everyone cheered. Pia blushed and shyly came to the middle of the group. She began her speech by thanking everyone for their gifts, and hoping they were all having a great time.

"Do you miss anyone, Pia?" Laura asked, smiling.

Pia smiled, and mentioned that she did miss her boyfriend Lorenzo, who could not come to the party as he was studying in Paris. She seemed a little sad, remembering her boyfriend.

As if on cue, the door to Laura's room opened slowly and a slim guy with long curly hair came out, beaming. Pia had her back to the door, so she did not notice the guy.

I looked at Laura. She winked at me.

Damn! So this was the surprise! Pia's boyfriend Lorenzo had decided to surprise Pia by coming to the party, all the way from Paris. And that is why Laura had asked Pia if she missed someone. She was setting the stage for Lorenzo. I wondered what tactic Laura would have applied if Pia had replied back saying she did not miss anyone. I couldn't help but chuckle at the thought.

Lorenzo slowly crept behind Pia and lifted her in his arms. Pia got startled at first, but then she shouted in delight when she saw Lorenzo.

"Oh my god! I don't believe this. You came all the way from Paris!!" Pia exclaimed, kissing Lorenzo.

"I wouldn't have missed your birthday for the world," Lorenzo replied, kissing her back.

Everyone started clapping and cheering. I couldn't help but smile at the amazingly romantic surprise. I glanced at Sofia, and I found her looking back at me. She was also smiling.

Laura turned on the music, a slow song this time, to match the romantic mood. We refilled our glasses, and started dancing. The party was in full swing.

Pia and Lorenzo had eyes just for each other. They kept smiling at each other, blushing and kissing passionately. After a few minutes, Pia discreetly took Lorenzo to her room.

"They won't come back out now," Laura said and I laughed.

After some time, Laura, playing the perfect host, decided to engage us further. She suggested that we play 'Spin the Bottle'. We all agreed.

The game started. The initial challenges were related to drinking. We would give the bottle a spin, and wait for it to stop. The person towards whom the bottle would point, once it stopped spinning, was asked to drink two shots of whisky.

As the game progressed, we all got at least two opportunities to take those shots. A poor guy had taken so many shots that he had to abandon the game in between and rush to the bathroom to puke. He didn't come back for a long time, and was found sleeping on the bathroom floor by Laura later.

Once we were all sufficiently drunk, the game turned to more challenging and interesting tasks. People were asked to seduce or kiss each other.

When my turn came, I was asked to kiss the most beautiful girl in the room. It was a no-brainer for me, though I was not sure if Sofia would be okay with me kissing her. I turned to my right towards Sofia and looked at her, silently asking with my eyes if I could kiss her. I did not speak any words, but Sofia must have understood. She blushed and nodded slightly. It was a very slight nod, but I got the hint. As soon as I saw the nod, I kissed her before she could react.

It was just a gentle peck on the lips, but Sofia's face was completely red. I guessed it was due to a combination of all the blushing and drinking. Her red cheeks complimented her red dress perfectly, and made her look even more radiant.

I couldn't stop beaming the rest of the time, even after the party ended and we all went back home. I didn't remember anything else from the rest of the party, because my mind was still stuck on that kiss.

I had a feeling that Sofia felt the same way about me. Or maybe it was just me being extremely optimistic. After all, Sofia had a habit of blushing most of the time. It had just been a peck on the lips, but that brief moment with Sofia meant the world to me.

18

At EPFL, work was as usual for the next few days. Onur kept a close check on my progress and didn't look very happy. I couldn't really blame him. I wasn't putting in even half of my usual amount of effort with my mind pre-occupied most of the time.

Sofia had her exams going on, so she was busy. I was sad to know that she would go back to Berlin in a couple of weeks. Her exchange semester was about to end. It might be years before we would get to meet again. And I had not even confessed my feelings to her.

While I was lost in my thoughts, I received an email from Onur. It seemed like the lab was organizing an informal get-together, so that the lab mates could get a chance to spend quality time with each other and bond better. It was the season of the FIFA World Cup, so everyone was going together to Satellite to watch the match and have a few drinks together.

Since I had always been busy travelling or partying, I welcomed this opportunity to spend some time with my lab mates, especially considering I had less than a month of internship left.

Football is the most popular sport in Europe, and FIFA World Cup is a big event. As a result, the bar was completely full that evening, and everyone was excited. I ordered a pizza and a beer. I had gotten used to having my pizza without ketchup by now, in the Italian style.

Onur was talking about the most impressive goals in the history of football. He was a football fanatic, and seemed super excited that day.

I, however, was still thinking about Sofia. She was going to leave Switzerland soon, and I still had not told her about my feelings. I was too scared to lose her by confessing my feelings to her, in case she did not feel the same. I really wished there was a way I could know about Sofia's feelings for me.

Seeing me a little lost, Onur asked me if something was wrong. I shrugged and tried to change the topic, but he didn't look satisfied. The crowd suddenly started cheering and he got diverted. Someone had scored a tough goal.

When the match got over, I quietly crept out of the bar and started walking towards the bus stop. The crowd inside was suffocating me, and I needed some quiet time to think more about Sofia. Damn! I would miss her so much when she leaves.

I heard someone behind me, and turned to find Onur following me.

"Hey," I waved at him. "It was so crowded inside, I just came out for some fresh air…" I mumbled rather unconvincingly.

"Well, me too. Let's have some fresh air together, shall we?" Onur said with a sweet smile. It was the first time that I had seen Onur smile. I had no idea he even had the capability to smile. 'Maybe drinks did that to Onur,' I wondered.

He made me sit down, and asked me what was going on in my mind. To my surprise, I started talking, and told him everything from the very beginning. How I had met Sofia, how much I liked her, and whether I was just making a fool of myself. I didn't know why, but I suddenly found it very easy to open up to Onur. It was probably because of the alcohol, or because Onur was being so sweet for the first time. Or probably because I really needed to talk to someone.

Onur was silent throughout. He let me talk, while he just listened. I had wanted to talk to someone for a long time, and I felt more relaxed after pouring out all my thoughts.

Once I was done talking, he looked at me thoughtfully. "Do you really like her?" he asked.

"I don't know. I think I do. I love talking to her. I love hanging out with her. Whenever I see her, I suddenly start feeling more cheerful. There is an innate desire in me to always keep her happy."

"Let me tell you a story," Onur said, pausing briefly. "This is from a different generation, much before you and I were born."

▼

Once upon a time, many years back, there was a guy called Mark who really liked a girl named Lucy in his mathematics class. He used to think about her all the time. Being very shy, he was afraid to tell her about his feelings. In fact, he could not even talk to her properly.

The university ended, and everyone went their separate paths. Lucy left the town to find some work in a major city.

Mark tried hard to find Lucy, but couldn't. Those were the days prior to the advent of mobile phones or social media.

Years passed. Mark finally traced Lucy through one of their common friends, but heard that she had got married and was settled now. Heartbroken, Mark did not try to contact her.

He went back to his home town and married a girl of his parents' choice. They had a son. But Mark was still always lost in his own world. He could never forget Lucy. As a result, he was never really able to truly love his wife. His wife tried to be patient with him at first, but then got tired of trying to live a life without love, and divorced him. Mark never remarried.

One day, Mark received a letter from an anonymous source, informing him that his childhood sweetheart had passed away due to cancer. The note invited him to the funeral. Mark was completely heartbroken. Filled with tears, he took the next train to the city to attend the funeral.

On reaching the funeral, he met Lucy's husband at the gate. The husband told Mark that he was the one who had sent that letter to Mark. He had written the letter anonymously as he wanted to see if Mark still thought about Lucy as his childhood sweetheart.

He handed Mark a diary, which had Lucy's handwriting on the cover. He told Mark that Lucy had given him the diary on her deathbed and asked him to hand it over to him. The husband had no idea that Lucy used to maintain a diary.

Mark went through the diary, and was filled with tears on reading the notes. It turned out that Lucy had loved Mark all her life. She felt Mark probably did not like her as he never talked to her properly. She did not know for sure if Mark liked her or not, and did not have the courage to tell him her feelings. In those days, it was inappropriate for a girl to approach a guy, and so she refrained from approaching him in case he did not feel the same way about her. She had got married but had never found joy in her married life. She did not have kids. While her husband loved her, Lucy only thought about Mark all the time.

On realizing what he had lost because of his shyness, Mark was filled with so much remorse and sadness that he could not eat or sleep for many days. His health started deteriorating. He lost a lot of weight, and soon got bedridden. He kept crying at night, taking Lucy's name again and again.

Having no motivation to live anymore, he did not survive for long. Mark breathed his last merely a couple of months after Lucy had died. He never let go of her diary, not even during his last few moments. He always kept the diary close to his heart. The diary was buried along with him, resting on his chest, his hands wrapped around the diary, his tombstone reading, "Some love stories are meant to be fulfilled in the afterlife."

▼

There was a very long silence as Onur ended his story. I was stupefied and did not know what to say.

Onur broke the silence after a while. "I think you should tell her. At least you would know where you stand," he advised. "It is much better than repenting later on. You do not want to be another Mark. You do not want to wait for the afterlife to fulfil your love story."

Onur did make sense. Sofia was going to leave in a few days anyway. If I didn't tell her now, I might never get the chance again. What did I really have to lose? The thought of Mark and Lucy and the life that they could have had together made me shiver.

I thanked Onur. He patted my back and helped me get up, accompanying me to the bus stop. He tried to smile at me, but there was a strange sadness about his smile. He seemed to be burning from the inside, though he was trying to act tough.

"By the way, how do you know this story?" I called out as Onur began moving back towards the bar. He was walking slowly, slightly hunched over. Almost as if he was extremely exhausted, drained of all his energy.

For a moment, I thought Onur was not going to answer. I decided to let it go. The bus had arrived, and I started moving towards the bus.

"Mark was my grandfather," Onur suddenly replied, without turning back. There was a touch of sadness in his tone. A touch of regret. Regret for Mark. Regret for Lucy. Regret for the grandparents he could never have.

At that moment, I knew my relationship with Onur had changed forever. I could never see him as the hard and strict Onur again. The wall between us had finally crumbled.

19

For the next couple of days, I thought long and hard about Onur's story. I had made up my mind. I was not going to end up as another Mark. I had to tell Sofia about my feelings, or else I would end up regretting my entire life. I had to at least give it a try.

The day Sofia's exams got over, I received a text message from her.

"There?" The message read. Sofia was enquiring if I was online at that moment.

I was so glad to see her message. I was about to reply with the usual "Yes", but I decided to be slightly more creative. I decided to drop a hint to Sofia about how I felt about her, albeit in a casual way.

Being a Harry Potter fan, the first reply that came to my mind was, "Always". I decided to make the reply even cheesier by adding a couple of words.

"For you, always," I finally texted her back.

I could see that Sofia had read the message, but she didn't reply instantly. A minute passed by, before she started typing. My heart was beating so hard that I could hear my own heartbeats.

After what seemed like an eternity, her reply came through.

"Wow! That was really good. Since when did you learn to flirt?" She texted, with a winking smiley, and a couple of her usual hearts.

Her hearts always made me blush.

Before I could reply, she sent another message. "Laura and I had a chat after our last exam today. We are thinking of planning a trip to Amsterdam, our last trip of the exchange season. That would also be a farewell for Laura, as she would leave for Vienna directly from Amsterdam. Will you be able to make it? I know you have your internship, but please try to come?"

A trip to Amsterdam! That sounded like a lot of fun. And maybe I could confess my feelings to her in Amsterdam itself.

Going for the trip would mean missing a few days of work, and I wondered if Onur would allow me to do that. Even though Onur had stopped acting strict with me since that evening at Satellite, he was still my manager.

"Pleeeeeease!!" Sofia wrote again. "It would be soo much fun!"

I smiled at her excitement, rolling my eyes. I decided to talk to Onur anyway. I peeked at his office window and saw him engrossed in his laptop.

I knocked on his door and asked him if he had a couple of minutes. Without looking up from his laptop, he motioned for me to sit down.

Hesitatingly, I told him about Sofia's message regarding the trip to Amsterdam, and my plan to confess my feelings to her during the trip. Onur was silent the entire time, his face unreadable.

I was expecting a few harsh words from him, when I saw something that made me almost fall off my chair with surprise. Onur smiled. So Onur could smile even when he was not drunk, I thought.

"I am glad for you, and I really hope your plan succeeds. You can take the entire week off. I will manage Hamza," Onur said.

I almost felt like hugging Onur at that very moment, but somehow controlled myself. I thanked him, and he started laughing at seeing the excitement on my face.

As soon as I exited his office, I saw another message from Sofia.

"There? Reply idiot! Are you coming or not? I am pleading so much, and you are not even replying."

I laughed, copied my previous message and sent it back to her. "For you, always."

"Yayyyyyyy!" Sofia wrote back, followed by countless hearts. "Let me tell Laura. This is going to be such an amazing trip."

'I hope so,' I thought. We chatted for a few more minutes and I asked her how her exams went. She had aced her exams, it seemed. Especially mathematics. "And all thanks to you," she wrote.

I blushed. Onur passed me at that exact moment to get a cup of coffee, and saw me blushing like an idiot. He laughed and gave me a thumbs up.

Sofia, Laura and I decided to meet later that evening at Sofia's place to plan the trip in detail. We looked up the ticket prices of trains, buses, and car rentals from Lausanne to Amsterdam.

We found a bus company called "Flixbus", which offered cheap transportation between cities in Europe. We read the reviews, and found most of them to be positive. The buses were comfortable and generally on time.

We found an overnight Flixbus at good prices, and booked three seats instantly.

We then checked for affordable accommodation, and looked at the hostel options in Amsterdam. Europe had student hostels in most good cities, which offered shared dormitories at good locations and cheap prices.

We decided we would spend three days in Amsterdam, which was more than enough to properly visit the city and get to know their culture. Laura mentioned that she had to go to Vienna for a day to conduct some field research for her thesis on Mozart, so she would leave a day early and go straight to Vienna. After spending a couple of days in Vienna, she would go back to Italy to her home university.

I would have wanted to visit Vienna as well, but I only had a few days of leave from Onur and didn't want to push him too much. Onur had only just gone soft; he could very well revert to his old form if he thought I was taking him for granted. In addition, Sofia was also not going to Vienna because she had some last minute formalities to finish for the completion of her exchange studies. And it did not make sense for me to go anywhere without Sofia.

We found a room for three people in Amsterdam near the train station, and booked the room for two nights. Sofia and I would start our journey back to Lausanne on the third night, so we didn't need a room for that night. The hostel had great reviews, and we seemed lucky to have found such a good room available.

Tickets and accommodation booked, I looked excitedly at Sofia and Laura, and saw my excitement reflected back in their shining faces.

It was going to be a really great trip!

20

We met at the bus stop near the Lausanne station at around 9 p.m. The Flixbus to Amsterdam was supposed to arrive around midnight, but we decided to meet a little before that to grab dinner.

We sat at the McDonald's near the Lausanne station bus stop and utilized the time to make an itinerary for the upcoming trip, in terms of the tourist spots we were going to visit.

Amsterdam was primarily famous for two things: weed and prostitution. Amsterdam had no law against weed, which meant people could actually have weed anywhere, even in front of a policeman. As a result, they had converted this into a special tourist attraction, by having shops all over the city selling weed inside brownies and cakes. Interestingly, the shops selling weed were called "coffee shops" in Amsterdam.

The other popular attraction in Amsterdam was the red light area. It was supposed to be the largest red light area in the world, attracting people from all over. Even if someone did not want to indulge in prostitution, just visiting this area in Amsterdam was said to be an experience in itself.

We decided that we would spend the first night exploring the Red Light District and will also try our hands at one of the "coffee shops" in the area. Visiting the Red Light District was actually Sofia's idea, which was quite surprising to me. I didn't think girls would have any interest in the such places. But considering the fame of the red light area, a trip to Amsterdam would not be considered complete without a visit there.

There were also other some other tourist spots to visit in the city. Amsterdam was also known for its museums. We decided to fit those over the next couple of days, depending on our schedule.

By the time our bus arrived, we had a decent idea of our plan for the trip. We did not plan everything as some trips are much more fun when left unplanned to some extent.

Our passports and tickets were checked before we were allowed to enter the bus. The bus was much more comfortable than we had thought it would be. The temperature inside the bus was warm, in contrast to the cold outside. There was also a toilet. I would have found it really difficult to imagine a toilet inside a bus, but there it was! And that too, a clean one!

The seats were very comfortable and there was decent leg space, which was a blessing for a tall guy like me. Being 6'3" tall, I always found leg space a problem in buses, flights or even cars.

We were all quite tired, and fell asleep as soon as we sat down. Amsterdam was going to be the last stop for the bus, so we did not have to worry about missing our stop.

Sofia placed her head on my shoulder to sleep, and my stomach just flipped over again. Her strawberry perfume filled my senses, and all I wanted to do was cuddle with her and play with her hair. But somehow, I forced myself to sleep.

The next day at Amsterdam was going to be a long and exciting day, and we needed as much energy as we could muster.

The bus ride was comfortable, and we didn't even realize when we had reached Amsterdam. The first thing we noticed as soon as we stepped out of the bus was the gush of cold wind in our faces. Damn! It was really cold. Imagine someone throwing a bucket-load of ice on your face. It was that cold.

I had only brought a normal jacket with me, as I did not think I would need a very thick one. I hoped that would suffice, especially if we were planning to roam around late at night. Which we would, considering that the real Amsterdam came alive only at night.

We went directly to the hostel where we had booked our room. The hostel was at walking distance from the station. It took us just fifteen minutes to reach the hostel. We were greeted by an old lady at the reception, who was polite and had a welcoming smile. She was tiny, and had difficulty walking. I guessed her age to be at least eighty years. She greeted us with cookies and hot coffee. She also offered us some homemade cakes.

"These are pure cakes, not like the ones you will get in the coffee shops," she winked, referring to the infamous weed brownies of Amsterdam. The cakes were absolutely delicious.

It seemed like she owned the hostel, and had put in all her efforts in decorating and developing the place. She probably lived alone, so the hostel was everything she had. The walls were painted with bright colours, and had family portraits of the lady everywhere. There were also a few portraits of what seemed like travellers who had stayed at this place. The lady really loved her guests, it seemed. And I could guess that her guests probably loved her too.

We had a sumptuous breakfast, thanks to the lady, and decided to take a nap to refresh ourselves further. Our room had a double bed and a single bed. I took up the single bed while the girls took up the double bed. In my wishful thinking mind, I wished I could have taken the bed with Sofia. 'Hopefully one day,' I thought to myself.

Our agenda for the day was supposed to start in the evening with a visit to the Red Light District, and it was going to be a long night. We decided to take a nap so that we could stay awake all night, enjoying the night life of Amsterdam.

Laura was the first to wake up, and she kicked us awake. It was around six in the evening but I was so sleepy that it took her all but pouring a bucket of cold water on me to wake me up.

Once awake, we soon freshened up and left the hostel. In contrast to the morning, the city was now super lively, filled with people laughing and talking.

I was quick to form a first impression of the city. Somehow, I felt there was a different aura to Amsterdam compared to the other European cities. The city was, for lack of a better word, "wild". I mentioned my observation to Sofia, and she completely agreed. The city had a vibe that made you want to lose all inhibitions and bring out your wild side. Probably that is why the city made so much money from the activities which were banned in most of the other countries.

We were hungry and quickly shared a large pizza at an Italian restaurant before finally reaching the famed Red Light District, which is called De Wallen.

I had been warned, but I was still in for a huge shock. The initial part of the area was filled with shops selling sex toys, with banners everywhere mentioning the times of the live sex shows.

This place was particularly known for its 'window prostitutes'. There were dozens of red-lit cabins with glass windows next to the streets, where one could see the prostitutes, smiling and winking at the passers-by. Most of the girls wore skimpy lingerie, which hardly covered their assets, while some were completely naked. Travellers, men and women alike, came from all over the world to Amsterdam for this unique sight.

You could walk through the streets admiring the naked girls as much as you wanted, for free. If you wanted to indulge in any services with the prostitute, you could bargain for the price with the particular girl. The price list, I could make out from the guys bargaining around, was around 50 euros for full service.

The girls were gorgeous, to say the least. Sofia and Laura couldn't help but admire the girls as well. Beauty was, after all, universal. I guessed only the most beautiful girls got the chance to secure a spot at one of the coveted windows.

After roaming around the area and checking out the windows, we decided to go for a brownie at one of the 'coffee shops'. Laura said that her friends back at EPFL had recommended The Bull Dog for the best weed brownies in Amsterdam, and we saw one just down the corner. The Bull Dog was for weed brownies what McDonald's was for burgers. It was a franchise with stores all over Amsterdam, and you could expect the same standard and quality of the weed brownies in any of the stores.

As soon as we entered the place, we were struck by an extremely strong smell of weed and other drugs. The smell was so overpowering that it took us a couple of minutes to get hold of our senses.

"Damn!" Laura whistled, smiling. I looked at Laura and couldn't help but laugh at her naughty look. Sofia, excited as well, rushed ahead to grab the menus from the counter.

I decided to go for the standard Bull Dog Brownie, which was just right for newbies who wanted to have a flavour of the life at Amsterdam without losing control over themselves.

Laura and Sofia decided to opt for the hash brownies, which were slightly stronger. Laura seemed to have done quite a bit of research on the various kinds of brownies available in Amsterdam, and had come prepared with a list.

The brownies were small in size, just like cupcakes. They tasted normal as well, though they smelled slightly different. When I mentioned this to Laura, she told us that the cakes do not have their effect instantly, but usually take around an hour to really hit us.

I had a sudden urge to pee, and went to look for the toilets. There was a long queue and the toilets were dirty, but I didn't mind. By the time I came back to our table, I saw Sofia devouring another cake.

I looked at Laura. "I tried to stop her, but she was adamant." Laura shrugged at me.

"Oh come on, you guys!" Sofia exclaimed. "We are on a holiday with people we really love, and have nothing to worry about. Let us enjoy the moment!" The raw excitement in Sofia's beautiful eyes was really amazing.

I looked at Laura, who was equally perplexed by Sofia's excitement. We smiled at each other, happy to see Sofia this way.

"Plus, I know you will take care of me even if I lose my senses, so why do I need to worry," Sofia whispered in my ear.

"For you, always," I whispered back, so close to her face that I wanted to kiss her right there.

The pub suddenly started playing "Despacito", one of our favourite Salsa songs. Sofia screamed with delight, got up and pulled me along to the empty space between the tables.

We started dancing. Oh, and what a dance it was! Somehow, that night, we were dancing wildly, without any inhibitions whatsoever. Maybe it was the brownie, or maybe it was the sense of being with Sofia in a wild city. Or maybe it was just an unknown sense of happiness. But, in that moment, I forgot everything else and danced with Sofia like there was no one else in the world. In that moment, nothing else mattered.

Seeing us, the pub started playing Salsa songs one after the other, and we kept dancing. I looked sideways to see Laura chatting animatedly with a young handsome man with long hair in a ponytail. She saw me looking at her and winked slyly. I smiled, winked back and turned my attention to Sofia.

By then, the brownie had started hitting me, and I was feeling extremely light-headed. I could see from Sofia's expressions that she was feeling the same too. My feet were dancing to the beats automatically now. I looked at Sofia to find her dancing crazily, completely lost in the world of Salsa.

I went closer to Sofia, placed my arms on her waist and started dancing one of our favourite combinations. Sofia placed her arms on my neck. Our bodies were moving around in waves, in perfect sync with each other. My senses were filled with Sofia's fragrance. Sofia's arms were still wrapped around my neck, her hands playing with my hair.

'This is the moment,' I thought. If I did not kiss Sofia now, I would regret it forever. I took one long look at Sofia, pulled her closer and kissed her. I kissed her hard. I was scared she would pull back, but she didn't. Instead, she slowly opened her mouth. What followed was the most passionate kiss I could have ever imagined. We completely gave in to each other, our mouths moving together, tongues stuck to each other.

After what seemed like an eternity, we broke apart. I looked at Sofia, who was smiling at me. Her face was completely red, the colour that suited her the best. I motioned with my head if she wanted to go somewhere private, and she nodded.

I looked back to where Laura was sitting, to find her busy making out with the ponytail guy. I smiled. She would be fine, I hoped. Laura was strong and could take care of herself.

Sofia and I stepped out of the pub and made our way back to our hostel room. Sofia held my hand all along the way, her head on my shoulders.

As soon as we reached the room, I pushed Sofia against the wall and kissed her with all the passion I could muster. Sofia kissed me back with equal passion. I kissed her mouth, her face and her neck, finally coming back to her mouth. My tongue played with Sofia's tongue, intertwined with each other.

We swiftly shifted to the bed. Sofia removed her dress and unbuttoned my shirt. She kissed my neck, followed by my chest, before going further down. I couldn't control myself from gasping with pleasure. What followed was a night of raw passion. A night I would remember till eternity.

21

I woke up first, to find Sofia sleeping peacefully in my arms. She looked calm and sweet. The more I looked at her, the more I fell in love with her.

I was still in shock over the night's events. So much had happened in the last few hours that it seemed like The Bull Dog had been a distant past.

Laura had still not arrived at the room. I assumed she had spent the night at her ponytail man's place. I would have been worried about her, but I knew Laura was more than capable of taking care of herself.

I looked again at Sofia, and smiled. I couldn't believe my eyes. I was holding the most beautiful woman in my arms.

My phone buzzed. I picked it up. It was a message from Laura. She would arrive in a couple of hours.

My movement seemed to have woken Sofia up, who opened her eyes and smiled at me. There were so many things I wanted to tell her. I wanted to pour out all my emotions for her. I wanted to tell her how much she meant to me. I wanted to tell her that this was not a one night stand for me. I wanted to make love to her every single night, and wake up with her sleeping in my arms every single morning. Unable to find the right words, I just stupidly looked at her face.

Sofia's eyes, however, told me that she had read everything going on in my mind, and she nodded in an understanding manner.

We got up, refreshed ourselves and made some breakfast. Our kind host had left us a plate full of delicious cakes, along with some orange juice and coffee.

Laura arrived, blushing and quite happy. She kept talking about Adam, the guy with the ponytail. He hailed from Budapest, which explained his naturally tall and muscular frame.

Adam had come to Amsterdam to attend a friend's wedding. Laura gave a vivid description of Adam's life and hobbies. Adam seemed like an exotic guy, with hobbies ranging from skiing to scuba diving. I was really surprised how much they had talked to each other, considering they had met just a few hours before. Laura really seemed to like Adam, and I was happy for her.

"Don't you want to spend some more time with Adam?" Sofia asked Laura.

"Oh, he had to go back to Budapest today. But we exchanged numbers so that we can stay in touch. He promised me he would visit me in Italy," Laura replied.

"And guess the best thing about Adam! He loves music as well. We had such a great discussion about Mozart yesterday night," Laura exclaimed cheerfully.

"You found time to discuss Mozart as well? Were you guys just talking the whole night or what?" I couldn't resist asking.

"Well, we did talk a lot, among other things," Laura said, blushing. Sofia and I laughed.

"So, what have you guys been up to? I saw you dancing last night, but you probably left early because I didn't see you later," Laura said.

It seemed like Laura had not seen us kissing in the pub, so she had no idea what had happened last night. I glanced at Sofia to check if we should tell Laura, but her eyes seemed to say that she wanted to keep this a secret for some time.

Gosh! I had really become an expert in reading Sofia's eyes! A good start, I was sure.

"Well, we were quite hungry, so we decided to grab something quick to eat before heading back. We didn't inform you because you were busy chatting with your Adam," I winked, placing special emphasis on "chatting". Laura laughed.

"Hunger reminds me, I am starving!" Laura said, suddenly noticing the breakfast and diving into the plate of cakes.

Since Laura was leaving that evening for Vienna, we decided to quickly get ready and take a look at the various museums in the city.

We started with Madame Tussauds, a museum known for look-alike wax statues of famous celebrities. We took a lot of time there because Laura decided to click pictures with every single wax statue present. There were statues of celebrities from across the globe. Among the Indian celebrities, I could see statues of Amitabh Bachchan, Aishwarya Rai, Salman Khan and a few others. The statue of Aishwarya Rai was very inappropriately created though – she looked more like

Rakhi Sawant. Probably the creator of the statue got confused between the two, I chuckled to myself.

Sofia knew each of the Indian celebrities by name, which really impressed me. I would not have been able to recognize a single German celebrity.

Next, we visited the Torture Museum in Amsterdam, which had depictions of the various ways in which people used to be tortured in the past. The museum stood as a reflection of the painful past, and a testimony to the cruel means of torture.

Some of the torture instruments, such as the "skull-cracker", were so terrifying that they sent shivers down my spine.

Sofia stood close to me during the tour, holding my hand the entire time. I could see the horror in her eyes. The kind and gentle Sofia could not even imagine how cruel people used to be in the past when it came to torturing others.

After the tour of the Torture Museum, we decided to take a break and have lunch. We found a good Dutch restaurant just down the street, and decided to go for it. We were all silent while having lunch, either because we were tired or because we were still horrified by the Torture Museum. For me, it was the former.

After lunch, we decided to visit the Heineken Museum, which celebrated the journey of the famous beer brand Heineken and gave the spectators a hands-on tour of beer-making. Heineken, which had its headquarters at Amsterdam, made one of the finest beers in the world.

At the end of the Heineken Museum tour, there was a tasting room where everyone was given two glasses of the original Heineken beer. The beer, for some reason, tasted much better than the Heineken that is sold in the market. It might just have been my mind playing with me, so I asked Sofia and Laura if they felt the same. They agreed.

To engage the audience, the bartender decided to play a game. He decided to test the audience's knowledge about Dutch and the history of Netherlands. He spoke some English words and asked the audience for the Dutch translation.

Sofia knew the translation of every English word he spoke, and won at least half a dozen glasses of beer as a result. I was quite astonished and wondered if she knew Dutch as well, but then I came to know that the Dutch and German languages are very similar to each other, with many common words.

Those extra glasses of beer were shared among all three of us, so we were all quite light-headed by the time we left the museum.

Laura had to leave for Vienna in a couple of hours. We decided to go back to our hostel so Laura could pick up her bags and we all could freshen up. After that, we went to the train station to drop Laura.

"Are you sure you want to visit Vienna and not Budapest?" I winked at Laura, dodging a playful punch from her in return.

We still had a few minutes before the departure of the train, so Sofia decided to make a quick rush for the toilet.

"Raj, I wanted to tell you something. I am sure you know that already, but Sofia really likes you, you know! And I can see that you like her as well. You might not have told me, but I am not an idiot. The chemistry between the two of you is very obvious," Laura confided in me when we were alone. "I am not an expert on relationships, but I have experienced quite a few. You two have something very special. Don't ever let her go, else you will regret it forever."

It was encouraging to hear a confirmation of my own emotions from Laura. I nodded. I had experienced Sofia's passion last night. I had seen how comfortable and close Sofia felt to me during the day while touring the museums. Sofia and I had a strong connection, and I was not going to ever let her go.

Sofia arrived, just as we saw Laura's train arrive at the station. We waved her goodbye and promised to stay in touch. Laura said she would keep sending us pictures from her travels.

I had become quite fond of Laura during these past few weeks, and it really saddened me to realize that I had no idea when I would get a chance to meet her again. Farewells are always tough, especially when you have to bid goodbye to a close friend.

I looked at Sofia to find the same thoughts reflected in her moist eyes. I gently put my arms around her, and she placed her head on my shoulder. We watched in silence as the train departed.

22

After leaving the station, we wondered what to do. Both of us were still saddened by Laura's departure. I suggested we take a boat ride on the peaceful canals of Amsterdam to lighten up our mood, and Sofia agreed.

It was a full moon night, with countless stars twinkling in the sky. A perfect night for a romantic canal ride in the romantic city of Amsterdam.

We bought two tickets from the ticket counter for a one-hour boat ride. The last boat was going to leave in a few minutes, and we were just on time.

Sofia was very quiet, and had hardly spoken a word since we had left the station. I initially assumed that she was saddened by Laura's departure, considering that Laura and Sofia knew each other from much before and had studied in the same class.

But I realized there was something else going on in her mind as well. She was deep in thought, as if she was contemplating something.

We stood near the rails as the boat started moving, admiring the sound of the water splashing against the boat. The atmosphere was really serene, and a cool breeze was blowing.

I put my arms around Sofia, and we stood quietly next to each other against the rails, neither of us speaking anything.

I really wanted to pour out all my feelings for her. We had spent a night together, but I still had not got the chance to confess my feelings to Sofia. I wanted her to know that it was not a one night stand. I really cared about her, and I wanted her to know that.

I did not know where to start. Sofia probably sensed my hesitation, and slowly stroked my chest with her fingers, almost as if she wanted to say that it was okay. She understood everything.

However, I did not want to leave space for any kind of misunderstanding. I remembered Onur's story, and did not want to make the mistake that Mark had made. I mustered up enough courage and finally started speaking.

Weirdly, once I started speaking, I lost all my inhibitions. It was almost as if a dam had suddenly fallen apart, releasing a flood of emotions that had been forcefully locked inside since eternity.

Sofia did not speak a word. She just listened. She listened as I told her how much I loved her. How I had fallen for her the moment I had first seen her. How I wanted to spend each and every moment with her. How much I loved her kind and gentle soul.

I just couldn't stop speaking. I told her I thought about her all the time. I told her how her words sent ripples through my heart, how her angelic smile was enough to make me forget everything else in the world and how her strawberry fragrance was enough to make me lose my senses. I wanted to spend my entire life kissing her and making love to her. Just hugging her made me forget all my worries.

I kept talking and talking, until I just couldn't talk anymore. There was a long moment of silence. Sofia still had not uttered a single word. We stayed wrapped in each other's arms, my fingers stroking her hair.

After a few minutes, Sofia slowly broke apart and picked up her purse from the floor. She put her hand inside the purse, and took out a diary. It was a small diary, something that could easily fit inside a purse without making it too bulky.

She handed me the diary, opened at one of the pages. Wondering what it was all about, I took the diary and slowly started reading the opened page.

Now, it was my turn to stay silent, as I started reading the diary. I was reading slowly, absorbing each and every word. I took a long time to finish reading the diary. Sofia was patiently watching me all along, trying to read my expressions.

When I finally finished reading, I looked at Sofia with moist eyes. The diary was filled with descriptions of all our meetings, right from the Bern trip.

"I met a handsome Indian guy today at Bern. He was very shy, but had a subtle charm about him..." began the page which Sofia had pointed to while handing me the diary.

The diary went on to describe all our meetings from her viewpoint, the words capturing all her emotions. It turned out she had felt the same way about me from the day we had first met, and had been wondering if I liked her or not.

We played volleyball today at the beach, and there was such a great chemistry between us... almost as if we are meant to be together...

Raj and I enrolled in Salsa classes together. Salsa is so much fun! I get to learn something new and exciting with Raj. While dancing with him, I sometimes feel he wants to say something to me, but is hesitant to express the same. Does he like me as well?

Raj kissed me today. We were playing truth and dare... and he was given the dare to kiss the most beautiful girl in the room. Raj thinks I am beautiful! I mean, I know I am beautiful. But Raj thought I was the most beautiful girl in the room. I am so happy today. I would have been so jealous if he had chosen some other girl to kiss. I wish that our kiss could have gone on forever...

Laura, Raj and I are planning a trip to Amsterdam. I am so excited to spend time with Raj in a different city. Our time to say farewell is coming close now. Raj has not mentioned anything about his feelings to me, and I am scared to confess my feelings lest I lose him as a friend...

We made love last night. Oh, and it was so wild! Raj kissed me like he wanted every bit of me, and I kissed him back with the same passion. Our souls united last night. I hope we make love like this every single night...

I looked up at Sofia, who was watching me intently, as if gauging my reaction. Her eyes were moist as well. She hugged me tightly, burying her head in my chest.

I raised her face, brought her closer to me and kissed her deeply. All our hidden emotions from the past few weeks melted together to create the most passionate kiss ever in the history of mankind.

We were lost in each other, two souls finally mingling into one. At that moment, we did not care about anything else in the world. That moment was nothing but divine.

We broke apart after ages, and Sofia buried her face in my chest again. I kissed her head, my fingers playing with her hair. Sofia's happiness was all I cared about now. Nothing else mattered to me. Nothing.

"I love you a lot, Raj. Promise me that you will be there for me." Sofia softly whispered.

"For you, always," I replied. I meant each and every word, from the bottom of my heart. I would always be there for her. Always.

The boat ride was about to come to an end, and we stayed wrapped in each other's arms, silently observing the starry sky. Deeply engrossed in each other's company, neither of us spoke a word for the rest of the ride.

23

There was just one week left before Sofia had to leave Switzerland and go back to Germany. She was done with her course now, and was busy with some last minute formalities. She had to give a presentation about her exchange experience at her home university, and sign a few documents to officially finish her studies.

However, the real challenge for Sofia would begin after all the formalities related to her course would get over.

Considering that Sofia wanted to pursue a course in film production after her graduation, she needed to secure a good internship related to film production so that she could gain some experience and justify her interest in the film production course.

Unlike India, where it was relatively easier to switch streams, it was difficult to change majors in Germany. Economics and film production were not related in any manner, and it was not going to be an easy shift for Sofia, from an academic and career perspective.

However, Sofia was determined and had already started looking for internships in major film production companies across the world. I didn't know the names of most of the production houses she had applied to, but she said those were the best production houses in the world. Sofia was really ambitious, so I wasn't surprised she wanted to intern with only the best.

I also had only a few days left in Switzerland, before my visa expired. I had to finish my project and give a presentation to Hamza before leaving. Onur had been very kind and helping, giving me extra time to help me catch up, especially after I returned from Amsterdam.

Onur perceived what all had happened in Amsterdam the moment he saw me. According to him, my face had a whole new kind of glow these days. He was very happy for me, and I could sense that the happiness and care was genuine.

I tried to spend as much time as possible with Sofia these days. We met every day, as soon as I got free from the lab and she got free from her classes.

We would either go out for a walk along the lake, choose a nice restaurant for a romantic dinner, or just spend the evening wrapped inside a blanket at Sofia's place, watching a movie.

Sofia informed me about a farewell being organized by the university for all the exchange students.

"You definitely need to come with me," she said. "It would be so much fun."

"I'm not sure. I won't know anyone there. Besides, I'm not even invited," I said. I wanted to accompany Sofia, but I didn't want to intrude.

"Oh we are allowed to bring our boyfriends or girlfriends along. So you're coming with me. Believe me, you'll enjoy a lot," she said and smiled.

I loved it so much when Sofia referred to me as her boyfriend these days, especially while introducing me to her friends. She wanted to let the world know that I was hers, and that she was mine. I was really lucky. I wished I could take Sofia to India and introduce her to my friends as well. I couldn't help chuckle at the thought of how jealous my nerdy IITian friends would be on meeting my gorgeous girlfriend.

"Okay, I'll come with you. When's the party?" I asked.

"Yayyyy! I love you so much. It's tomorrow evening," Sofia said happily, kissing me with delight.

The next day passed by with me doing nothing productive in the lab. Even though I had to prepare for the upcoming presentation with Hamza, my mind was always on Sofia these days. I hated the fact that she was going to leave soon, and then it would be so tough for us to meet regularly.

What if she finds someone else when she goes back to Germany?

That was my greatest fear, and I couldn't even imagine losing Sofia. As I left the lab to go to my room that evening, I promised myself I would do all it takes to ensure I always keep Sofia happy.

I wanted to look really good tonight, for Sofia. I shaved off my rough stubble, took a long bath and put on my best clothes. I decided to wear a leather jacket that I knew Sofia loved.

I reached her place in the evening, a few minutes before the party. Sofia opened the door, and I was left speechless.

She was wearing a stunning blue sleeveless dress with high heels. The dress showed just enough of her cleavage to accentuate her figure. She was also wearing a thin necklace and big silver earrings. She had left her blonde hair loose and inclined to one side. She looked so gorgeous that my jaw just dropped open.

She laughed. "I know. I look great. Since it seems like you cannot get any word out of your mouth now."

I smiled. "I don't think I can even find a word to describe you right now. Such a word probably doesn't even exist in the dictionary."

Sofia blushed. "Well, you don't look half as bad either," she winked. "I am so glad you wore this jacket. I love it so much!" Sofia said, gently stroking my jacket.

"How much time do we have before the party starts?" I asked, slowly sliding my fingers on her arm, bringing my face close to hers.

"Shush! I don't want to ruin my makeup." Sofia pushed me apart. "Let us leave now. We are getting late."

"Oh come on! Just one kiss," I pleaded.

"Noooo!! Later! After the party," Sofia laughed, pushing me away.

We went outside and boarded the bus towards EPFL. The party was being organized near the lake. In fact, the party was at the exact location where the bar-be-que that Sofia and I were supposed to visit after our Bern trip had happened.

I couldn't resist glancing at Sofia sideways in the bus. She looked drop-dead gorgeous. She looked at me, smiled and blew me a kiss. I smiled back. I needed to keep reminding myself how lucky I was.

We soon reached the party. There were only around twenty people there, which meant we were very early.

Sofia waved to her friends, and introduced me to them. I always had difficulty remembering names. With so many people telling me their tough-to-pronounce names one after the other, I did not even try to remember them. I was probably not going to meet them again after that night anyway.

It was a lovely spot with a serene surrounding. There was a bonfire in the middle, and some people were standing around it. Other people, presumably the hosts of the party, were frying bacons on the bar-be-ques at one end.

My inhibitions about not knowing anyone were expelled very soon as I started talking to Sofia's classmates, who were extremely welcoming. "Ah! It feels good to finally meet you, Raj. Sofia keeps talking about you all the time," I heard from so many of Sofia's friends. It felt good to know that Sofia talked about me to her friends so often, even when I was not around.

Somebody took out a crate full of beer bottles, and we distributed the bottles among the group.

The party progressed and we were all having a great time eating and drinking. Somebody got out speakers and put on music. It was not long before we were all completely drunk, jumping and dancing around. A bunch of friends celebrating all the good memories from their exchange. Students from all corners of the world, celebrating together one last time before going back to their respective countries.

I asked Sofia if she wanted to dance with me. She readily agreed, stood up and put her arms around my neck. I held her by her waist and we started dancing to the music.

"I will miss everyone so much when I go back. This exchange was the best thing that ever happened to me," Sofia said sadly.

"I am sure you all will keep meeting each other in reunions. You have friends all over the world now," I said, trying to cheer Sofia up. She brightened up a little.

"Thanks for inviting me to the party. I love this," I said to Sofia while dancing.

Sofia smiled. "I'm glad you came too. It wouldn't have been half as much fun without you."

The music being played was a very soft melody, the kind of music meant for slow romantic dances.

As we slowly moved with the music, Sofia came closer to me and placed her head on my chest. I absolutely loved it when she did that. I could feel her fingers slowly moving down from my neck to my waist.

I was getting turned on, and I was sure Sofia could feel that. I had a sense Sofia was deliberately turning me on. I could sense her smiling, as her hands played around with me. I tried hard to control my boner, but it had a mind of its own. Sofia knew exactly how to turn me on, and she was at her best today evening.

As the dance progressed, I could feel the sexual tension in the air. There was a gentle breeze, and Sofia's hair was on my face. Her face was very close to mine, our cheeks brushing against each other.

As we danced with our bodies touching each other, Sofia slowly started moving her body against mine. She moved her body in slow circles against mine, knowing exactly where to make our bodies touch. After a few minutes, I couldn't control anymore and lifted Sofia's face up. Not caring about her makeup anymore, I kissed her hard. Sofia, instead of resisting, opened up to me. We kissed hard, our tongues interlocked, without worrying about the dozens of students around us.

After what seemed like hours, we finally broke apart. The music was still on. Some people were still dancing while others were lying around on the ground in a drunken state.

I looked at Sofia. She was smiling and blushing at the same time, just in her usual way. We left the party, and went to Sofia's place. She took me straight to the bedroom. She asked me to wait there and went to the bathroom.

I looked around, and saw a couple of suitcases lying around. Sofia had already started packing, and that saddened me. My thoughts, however, were broken when the bathroom door opened after a few minutes and I saw Sofia standing there. She was completely naked, her blonde hair ruffled just perfect enough to add to the beauty. I gaped at her for a few seconds, before rushing towards her, grabbing her and kissing her with all the passion I could muster.

I picked her up, and threw her on the bed. I then took off my clothes as well, jumped on the bed on top of her and started kissing her again.

Sofia turned me over, and started kissing my neck. She used her tongue to play with my body, moving her tongue in slow circles around my neck. She then slid her tongue down to my chest and started kissing me all over.

I was out of control by now, gasping with pleasure. She then slowly started moving further down. "Oh Sofia," I cried. It was pure ecstasy. A few seconds later, I turned her over. I licked her breasts, then kissed her stomach, before going further down on her. I could see that she was enjoying it, because she held my hair to stop me from moving away, with her body convulsing with pleasure.

After a few seconds, she opened her drawer to search for a pack of condoms. She took one out and helped me put it on.

I placed myself on top of her and gently entered her. She pulled me closer and kissed me passionately as we made intense love.

24

"Wake up, honey!"

I opened my eyes to find Sofia sitting on the bed beside me, holding a cup of coffee.

I sat up and thanked her for the coffee. "Last night was so damn perfect!" I exclaimed.

Sofia laughed, but seemed lost. I asked her if something was bothering her.

"I'm leaving for Berlin tomorrow, and you'll also leave for India in a few days. I wish we could have spent more time together," Sofia said sadly.

I had been thinking the same. What Sofia and I had was really special, and I did not want that to end. I had heard that long distance relationships had a lower success rate than normal relationships. And when the distance spans across countries and time zones, well, that could pose a problem. However, I was sure we would manage somehow. Or so I hoped. Sofia meant the world to me now, and I was ready to do anything to be with her.

"I'm sure we would figure something out. I will always be with you." I smiled at her and hugged her. Sofia smiled as well, though it was a slightly forced smile, her mind still occupied with the worry.

I spent the entire day with Sofia, helping her pack her suitcase and finish all the last-minute formalities such as cleaning the flat, and then inviting her landlord for an inspection of the flat before leaving.

In Europe, the landlords take some money from the tenants as deposit when they check in. It is very important to leave the flat as clean as possible while checking out, otherwise the tenants could stand the risk of losing their deposit.

Some of Sofia's friends came over to say goodbye. They sat there for a few minutes and had some beer, before realizing that Sofia actually just wanted to be left alone with me during her last few hours in Switzerland.

On the eve of her departure, we went to a fancy restaurant for a private dinner. We ordered the best wine they had, neither of us worrying about the expenses that evening. All we wanted was to make our last evening together in Switzerland as memorable as we could.

We ate, drank, talked and laughed. We became nostalgic and remembered all the amazing times we had during the past few weeks. We remembered all the travels, the Salsa dance classes and even our little picnics.

Almost as if on cue, the restaurant started playing a Salsa song. It was a slow Salsa song, unlike the usual fast ones. "Do you want to dance?" Sofia asked me, her eyes knowing fully well I would say yes.

"Of course, Sofia," I replied, holding her hand and helping her get up. We started dancing to the slow song, reminiscing all those previous memories through our slow and sensual Salsa moves. We were completely lost in each other's eyes, just dancing to the song. The restaurant owner saw us engrossed in Salsa, and started playing Salsa songs one after the other.

We kept dancing, not paying any heed to the dozen other people in the restaurant who were watching us with admiring eyes. We kept dancing, not paying any attention to the fact that the expensive food we had ordered had become cold now. We just kept dancing. Two bodies, moving together in perfect sync. That night, the restaurant saw the best dance performance ever. It was not just two people dancing. The restaurant that night saw the culmination of two lovers. Two souls merging into one.

As I accompanied Sofia to the airport the next day, it took me all my strength to keep myself from breaking down. I glanced at her. She looked gorgeous even in a simple casual T-shirt. The only difference being her missing smile. As we sat next to each other in the train to the airport, all we could do was just stare at each other's eyes, as if we wanted to save each bit of the other person's features in our memory forever.

We didn't speak a single word in the entire journey. We just held each other's hands, our hearts beating together, our eyes doing all the talking. We had no idea when we would meet each other again, and we did not want to let go of each other's hands.

As it happens, time always passes crazily fast when we want time to freeze. Before we realized it, we had reached the airport. As we stopped near the point after which visitors were not allowed, Sofia turned and hugged me hard. I hugged her back, and we just stood like that until it was time for Sofia to go. I breathed hard, taking in her rich strawberry fragrance, knowing fully well I would miss that fragrance so much. I removed her blonde hair from her face and kissed her lips.

Sofia took one last look at me, before turning around and entering the airport. There were no goodbyes, just an understanding and hope that we would meet again.

I stood transfixed for some time as I watched her go, not knowing what to do. It seemed like someone had just placed a heavy rock on my heart. I so wished I could simply leave everything and accompany her inside the airport at that very moment.

With moist eyes and a heavy heart, I turned around and started walking towards the train station. I felt empty, as if I had left a part of myself behind. However, deep inside my heart, I felt and hoped Sofia and I would meet again soon.

25

I could not concentrate on work. Sofia had already left for Germany, and I would need to go back to India in a week's time. I would have to resume my college studies at IIT Kanpur, so there was no way I could extend my stay in Europe at the moment.

Onur passed by my cubicle for a cup of coffee, and saw me engrossed deep in thought, with a forlorn look on my face. He came over and sat beside me, giving me that welcoming smile which propelled me to pour out all my feelings without any inhibitions.

Somehow Onur had become my closest confidante in the past few days. Considering how we had started when I had first set foot inside the lab, I was still surprised at this massive and completely unexpected turn of events.

Onur listened patiently and nodded in an understanding manner. He did not interrupt, and listened to the entire story patiently. After I finished speaking, he was silent for a few minutes, as if he was searching for a solution.

"Why don't you visit her in Berlin?" asked Onur.

"I still have to finish my project," I said, reminding Onur about the presentation that I had to give Hamza at the end of my internship in a week's time. "And then I have to leave for India to finish my studies. I cannot stay in Europe forever, you know. At least, not until I finish my studies first," I said.

"I am sure we can figure something out. I will talk to Hamza and re-schedule your presentation to a time slot as early as possible. Maybe day after tomorrow, if you can be ready by then. You will be completely free after that, to go wherever you want." Onur smiled.

I could not believe my ears. This seemed like an excellent solution, and I could not believe Onur would do that for me. Preponing my presentation meant Onur would have to speak to Hamza about me and make up some excuse. I could not understand why Onur would go to all that trouble for me, especially because it might also put Onur's position at risk if Hamza caught the excuse.

"Onur, I have no idea how I can ever thank you for all that you have done and are still doing for me," I couldn't help saying. I meant each and every word. Onur had played a critical role in ensuring Sofia and I could be together. And even now, he was still going out of his way to ensure Sofia and I could still remain together. He was just my internship mentor after all, and did not need to do any of this.

"Don't worry, buddy. Just go and get your girl. Seeing you so happily in love is reward enough for me," Onur smiled, his eyes deep in thought.

I wanted to hug Onur right then and there, but somehow controlled myself. There were other people present in the lab, and Onur had an image to maintain. He wouldn't want the other lab mates to know that there was a tender heart behind the brutal Hitler.

I had a feeling there was more to Onur's past than just the story he had told me about Mark. Did Onur also have an unfulfilled love story? Is that why Onur was so ruthless to everyone at the lab, because he wanted to hide the pain inside him? Is that why he wanted to help me so much, so that I did not have to live through the same pain? Something told me Onur did not want to discuss his past anymore, and I did not prod him.

As promised, Onur talked to Hamza and preponed my presentation. For the next two days, I worked my ass off to finish all my work in just two days. Considering that I had a tight deadline, Onur and the other lab mates also helped me as much as they could.

The next two days went by in a haze, between working till late evening in the lab, and spending the night talking to Sofia via skype. Sofia was missing her exchange days. Having spent so much time in Switzerland, she found going back to her normal life in Germany a significant change.

We would keep talking until one of us slept. Most of the times, it was Sofia who slept first. Just looking at her, even if it was through skype, and knowing that she was mine, made me feel extremely warm from inside.

I did not inform Sofia that I would soon be done with my internship and could join her in Berlin. I wanted to surprise her by unexpectedly visiting her in Berlin. Again, one of Onur's ideas, who helped me wherever I lacked in romantic imagination.

The two days went by, and the day of my presentation finally arrived. I had finished my project by pulling an all-nighter the night before, and was ready for the presentation.

I reached the conference hall just in time to find Onur waiting for me there. "Hey buddy! Just wanted to wish you good luck before the presentation. I'm sure you'll do well," Onur winked and smiled, before accompanying me inside the room. He had probably sensed that I was nervous, and his greeting really helped in soothing me down.

I began the presentation by introducing the project and the approach I had taken to solve the problem. Once I began speaking, I forgot all nervousness. It was my project, and I had worked hard on it, especially on the last two days. I had given many presentations in the past, and I knew how to ace presentations. I was in my best form today, explaining the approach and steps taken in detail, showcasing my depth of understanding.

There were a few questions from Hamza in between, and some from Onur. Onur's questions were more of a customary nature, and were quite easy. He was asking questions primarily for the sake of asking, fulfilling his duty as my internship mentor. Hamza's questions were really hard, and I struggled on a couple of the questions. Overall, the presentation went quite well, though.

At the end of the presentation, Hamza thanked me for the project and for being such a great intern. I thanked Hamza for giving me this opportunity, and to all the lab mates for the constant support. I had not thought about this before, but I had become quite used to the lab and the Ph.D students by now. I would miss the lab mates once I went back. Especially Onur. 'Yes, especially Onur,' I thought to myself, still surprised at how things had turned out between Onur and me.

Once everyone left, I decided to go for one last lunch with my lunch squad. I had not been able to spend time with them over the past few days, because I had been busy with Sofia and with the project. I wanted to properly meet them one last time and say goodbye. They had been my first friends when I had arrived in Switzerland, and I would miss them a lot. They had helped me immensely in settling down in this new country, especially during my initial few days here.

The lunch group was in full attendance that day. I had mentioned to them before that this would be my last lunch at EPFL, and the group had organized a small farewell for me. Manu, Vasia, Samuelle and the others were all sad on knowing that I was leaving so soon. They had ordered a farewell cake for me, with the caption "Never say farewell, Raj," on the cake.

Just seeing the cake brought tears to my eyes, as I remembered all the memories with them. I was also hit by a pang of guilt for not having spent enough time with them in the past few days. And I knew I could not change that now. I could only promise to meet them again soon, whenever I was around.

With a heavy heart, we bid our farewells, each of us knowing very well that the chances of us meeting again anytime in the near future were very slim.

26

Once I left EPFL for the last time, I made a stop at the nearby mall to buy a gift for Sofia. I wanted to surprise her with a romantic gift, but I did not know much about buying gifts for girls, so I decided to try my best.

After searching for a couple of hours for the ideal gift, I found a stunning black backless dress. It would look perfect on Sofia. Just picturing her wearing that dress and looking drop-dead gorgeous made me excited.

I had booked train tickets to Berlin for tonight. I was so overwhelmed with excitement that I was almost shaking. I had never done something this crazy in my entire life, and the adrenaline rush was making me restless. I simply could not wait to see Sofia's expression when she would open the door to find me standing outside.

I caught some sleep in the train. I had requested a co-passenger to wake me up when we reached Berlin, and he had been kind enough to oblige. I had also set up an alarm a few minutes before the time when I was expected to reach Berlin, but I wanted to be sure, just in case.

While sleeping in the train, I saw Sofia in my dreams. This is probably because my mind was so occupied with Sofia at the moment, that the dreams just accentuated the thoughts in my mind. She was wearing the black dress that I had bought for her, and looked radiant. We were together, and happy. *Very soon, the dream would become a reality.*

On reaching Berlin, I took the metro and went straight to Sofia's place. She had once told me, a long time back, where she stayed in Berlin, and I somehow still remembered that. Probably because she had told me she lived right next to the famous tourist location called Checkpoint Charlie, and because her flat number was 7, which was also the favourite number of each Harry Potter fan, as it happened to be the most magical number in the world.

It was at such moments that I was really grateful for my strong memory. Sofia would have become suspicious if I had asked for her address, and my surprise might have gone waste. There was nobody else I could have contacted to get her address either.

When I reached near her apartment, I took out my cell phone to check my reflection on the screen. I took a look at my hair to see that it looked okay. I was nervous, and wanted to look my best. Once I was sure I looked as good as I could, I rushed up the stairs to her apartment and rang the bell.

I was shaking with excitement as I waited for the door to open. After a few minutes, Sofia opened the door, and her jaw dropped open. She stared at me for some time as if she couldn't really believe I was actually there. She probably thought I was a fragment of her imagination, and just stood transfixed.

I savoured the moment for a few minutes, before finally breaking her out of her trance. "Hey!" I smiled. Sofia was still surprised, but a big smile slowly lit up her face. She rushed forward, jumped and gave me a huge hug, wrapping herself around me, her feet crossing against my waist. I kissed her wildly, and she kissed me back with so much force that it almost made me fall backward.

She took me inside her flat and showed me around. It was a nice and cosy flat, with wallpapers of different shades, from blue to pink. There were also posters on the wall depicting motivational quotes from books or movies. I smiled when I recognized one of my favourite quotes from Harry Potter, "It is our choices, Harry, that show what we really are, far more than our abilities."

'Well, I had surely made my choice well,' I thought to myself, looking fondly at Sofia.

There were also a few photos on the wall of Sofia with her friends and family. She showed me a few photographs of her childhood and asked me to recognize her from among all the kids. I squinted at all the blonde girls in the picture, trying to recognize her. It took me a few seconds, but I got it right in my first attempt. Sofia was impressed.

"People say I have changed a lot from my childhood days. I am quite surprised you were able to recognize me," Sofia said.

"Your cheeks are still the same. Cute and red," I winked. Sofia blushed, and her cheeks turned red. Ah! I had missed that blush so much in the past few days.

"Wait, I have something for you. Close your eyes." I wanted to show Sofia the dress that I had bought for her. She closed her eyes, smiling and waiting for the present.

She looked so beautiful while standing there with her eyes closed, that I couldn't help just staring at her.

"Oh hello! Are you going to show me something or not? I can't contain my curiosity further," Sofia said.

I laughed, and took out the dress I had bought for her. I asked her to open her eyes and she jumped with excitement when she saw the dress. "Oh my god! It's lovely. Thanks so much!" Sofia exclaimed. "I didn't know you had such a good taste in dresses," she teased me.

"Well, I don't know about that, but I do know I have a great taste in girls," I winked. "Why don't you try this dress on?"

"Why don't you help me in trying on the dress?" she said in a playful tone, slowly taking off her T-shirt and shorts. She was not wearing any undergarments.

This time, it was my jaw that dropped open. She looked drop-dead gorgeous, as usual.

"I am waiting for you to help me with the dress," Sofia said with a wide seductive smile.

"I think the dress can wait," I replied. She laughed.

I pulled her towards me and kissed her hard. She kissed me back. She then removed my clothes, took me to the bathroom and opened the shower. The water was cold, and that made me come closer to Sofia.

What followed was an intense session of lovemaking in the shower. Both of us had been longing for each other, and the longing came out in the form of the wildest sex I could have ever imagined.

I could not remember the last time when I was so happy and satisfied. I could only wish that this happiness would last forever. I had found the perfect partner in Sofia, someone I could really relate to as a whole. My life felt complete whenever I spent time with her. I had heard that love can make you go crazy, but it felt really weird to see that actually happening to me.

Life was just perfect. As perfect as I could have ever imagined it to be.

27

I woke up to find Sofia still wrapped around my arms, her head resting on my chest. She was sleeping, and I could not help but just look at her peaceful face. I noticed her eyebrows flickering slightly, and wondered what she was dreaming about.

I kissed her on the forehead. Sofia shifted her head slightly and adjusted herself to a more comfortable position on my chest. It was all I could do to stifle a laugh. I kissed her on the forehead again. She shifted more this time, almost waking up, before going back to sleep.

Her head's movement on my chest made me tickle, and I burst out laughing. Sofia woke up with a start, clueless about what just happened.

"Good morning, pretty girl," I said, still laughing hard. Sofia, confused and sleepy, grunted something which sounded like "fuck off" and went back to sleep – this time with her head resting on the pillow.

I smiled and checked the time. We were so tired that we had slept through the entire morning. It was almost noon.

I went to the kitchen to make some coffee. The kitchen was clean and well organized. I was not used to such a clean kitchen. Even the kitchen at my home was not so organized.

I looked around for coffee and found a box on the shelf after a few minutes of searching. The label said that the coffee was of Hazelnut flavour, something I had never tried.

I took my own time in preparing the two cups of coffee, as I kept thinking about Sofia and my future. I had only a couple of days before I had to leave for India. After that, I had a year to go before I finished my B.Tech. Sofia would probably start her film production course next year once she was done with her internship, assuming she got an internship soon.

I could either try to shift to Germany for a Master's, or try to search for a job in Germany after my B.Tech. But my choice would also depend on the country where Sofia would finally get her job.

Sigh! There were so many variables to consider in a long distance relationship across continents. It would be very difficult for her to settle down in India, so I will have to be the one to shift. I was quite used to European ways by now anyway.

I heard Sofia wake up, and went to her room with the coffee. She smiled on seeing me bring the coffee, and blew me a kiss.

"Will you make coffee for me like this every morning?" Sofia asked.

"There is nothing more I would like to do all my life, pretty girl," I said, longing for such a life.

As I sat down on the bed beside her, she reached out for her cell and started checking her emails. A few seconds later, she screamed so loudly that I almost spilled my coffee in shock.

I looked at Sofia to see her staring at her phone in delight, a wide smile plastered on her face.

"What happened?" I asked with surprise, wondering what could be such a good news.

"I got selected for a film project at Tel Aviv. I just got my acceptance letter. I will be assisting the producer on a film that is being shot in Israel. I cannot believe this. I had applied just to try my luck. I never really thought I would actually get this role. I mean, I don't even have any film background. This is so amazing I can't believe this," Sofia replied, her tone so unsteady with shock and delight that I had difficulty understanding her completely.

I made Sofia repeat the entire thing again to ensure I had heard it properly, and then hugged her tight. I was very happy for her. The way she spoke about this film company, it seemed to be a really famous firm.

"I am so proud of you. This is such great news. You can leverage this experience to gain further foothold into the world of films. They must have been really impressed with your application to select you without any film background," I cheerfully told Sofia. She nodded in agreement, still hugging me.

"Oh Raj, I am so excited!" Sofia said, suddenly shrieking again. I laughed hard at seeing her so delighted.

"So when do you start this assignment at Tel Aviv?" I asked Sofia.

"Oh, I completely forgot to check the dates in my excitement," Sofia said, breaking apart to check her email again.

"They want me to come there in a couple of weeks. There will be a few training sessions as soon as I reach, after which I will directly start assisting the producer. The entire project will take around half a year," Sofia said, reading the email.

Sofia read the email further to check more details about the project. It was supposed to be a panoramic perspective of the various traditions and cultures in Israel. That sounded interesting to me, and would probably involve immense learning. Sofia was excited that she would probably get to travel to many local places and live with the locals to really explore the culture. She loved exploring the local food and traditions wherever she went.

"We should celebrate. This is a big achievement. Let's get ready and go out somewhere," I said cheerfully.

"Right now?" Sofia asked, surprised.

"Why? Do you have other ways in mind to celebrate?" I teased Sofia, bringing my hand closer to her stomach to tickle her.

"Wait Tiger! Save your stamina for later tonight." Sofia laughed.

"So, get ready then. Let's get out from the house and then figure out what to do," I said.

"But I want to sleep more," Sofia said, stifling a yawn.

"Oh really?" I said, bringing my hands close to her stomach again until she burst out laughing.

"Okay okay let's go out. But give me some time to get ready first," Sofia said, still laughing.

We took some time getting ready. Sofia wore the black dress that I had gifted her, and looked like an angel. The dress fit her perfectly, accentuating her figure at all the right places. I was proud of my choice – for the dress as well as for the girl wearing the dress.

"So where are we going?" I asked Sofia.

"What? You made me get ready in a hurry to go out, but you don't even have a place in mind where we can go?" Sofia teased me.

"Well, it is your city. I will leave it up to you to choose the place. It will be an insult to you if I choose the place while you are here," I said. "I am starving though, so we should get some lunch somewhere, maybe?"

Sofia agreed, and said she knew just the perfect place for lunch. A place by the name of Alex's Cuisine Land, which was apparently considered among the best places in the city for lunch.

Out of habit, I took out my cell phone to search for the bus route to the place. "What are you doing?" Sofia asked.

"Just checking the bus route to Alex," I replied.

"You are in my hometown. I have a car, you idiot," Sofia laughed.

"Ah! Yes, of course you have a car," I said, mentally kicking myself for not guessing that. I had forgotten that most students in Europe had their own car. I accompanied Sofia to the garage. I whistled when I saw her car. Mercedes Benz C class!

"Damn! How rich are you?" I couldn't help asking, completely surprised.

"Ha-ha! Not that rich. It is second hand. One of the few possessions I have. Come on, let's go," Sofia said.

I still couldn't believe I was dating a girl who drove a Mercedes Benz C Class, even if it was a second hand car. That car was a dream car for so many of my friends. I never had a great interest in cars, but even I knew that this was a great car. So Sofia also had a great taste in cars! The more I got to know about Sofia, the more perfect she seemed, I couldn't help observing.

The drive to Alex was a short and comfortable ride. Alex was a cosy restaurant, well known for its lunch buffet. The buffet menu consisted of dishes ranging from plain croissants to hamburgers and pizza slices.

We chose a table outside the restaurant, to enjoy the view of the street. We were silent for a few minutes, completely engrossed in the food.

Right across the street, there was a shop selling sex toys. I couldn't help blushing at the posters outside the shop, showing various types of masturbation enhancement toys.

Sofia noticed me blushing at seeing the shop, and started laughing. "My baby is okay having wild sex, but blushes when he sees a shop selling sex toys?" Sofia teased.

"Not really. It's just that I am not used to seeing such posters and sex toy shops in public in India," I said.

"Do you want to visit the shop and buy something?" Sofia teased me again.

"No thanks. Anyway, I will leave for India in a couple of days. What will I do with those toys there? Unless you have some plans to use these toys tonight…" I teased Sofia.

Sofia laughed. "Toys have never been my thing. I have tried them a few times, but they are not even close to the real experience."

I had no idea how to react to that, considering I had no experience with sex toys at all.

"Maybe one day, we will try them together. Who knows, I might like them if used with the right guy," Sofia added, making me blush.

"One day for sure," I replied, smiling sadly, wondering when that day would arrive once I return to India.

Sofia saw my sad expression, and asked me if I wanted to go to the cinema with her to watch a movie tonight. "But won't all the movies be in German?" I asked.

"Yes, but a few of the movies are also in English. Some of us do understand English also, you know," Sofia teased me. I laughed.

Sofia checked the timings of the English movies, and booked tickets for a night show. We still had a couple of hours to kill before the movie. So once we were done with the lunch, we decided to take a peaceful stroll in Volkspark Friedrichshain, one of Berlin's oldest parks.

The weather was calm, and the lush greenery all over the park made the weather even better. There was a cool wind blowing in our faces.

In a few designated areas of the park that were not completely covered by trees, there was some sunshine. I was quite surprised to find a few people, both men and women, sunbathing completely naked in the park. *Completely naked!* Sofia saw my expression, and explained how this was quite common in Germany. Germany was known for its nudist culture, and many Germans practised this culture regularly. As a result, you could find many parks and hot water baths populated by nudists, relaxing without any care in the world.

"Wow," I said to Sofia, in a tone of disbelief. I couldn't even imagine something like this happening in India.

We took a full round of the park, enjoying the pleasant weather. Lost in each other's company, neither of us spoke much during the walk.

"I think we should leave for the movie now," Sofia said after some time, looking at her watch.

"Whatever you command, my queen," I replied, ducking a playful punch from Sofia.

Sofia drove us to the cinema hall. "So which movie are we watching?" I asked Sofia.

"*The Grand Budapest Hotel*," Sofia replied. "It is a recent German comedy movie which has become really popular all over the world. They have an English show once a day." I had heard of the movie. It had apparently taken the world by storm, winning multiple international awards.

We reached the cinema hall just in time for the movie to start. Sofia had booked the VIP couple tickets for us. As a result, we were allotted a large couch towards the back of the movie hall. I had heard of such couple couches, but I had never experienced one. Sofia smiled on seeing how pleasantly surprised I was.

As soon as the movie started, I knew I would not be able to concentrate on the movie at all. With the lights dimmed for the movie, Sofia came closer to me on the couch, her head resting on my shoulder. As usual, my senses were completely overwhelmed by her strawberry fragrance.

Sofia slowly started sliding her right hand down my chest, her fingers playing with my body. She was trying to turn me on, and my body was obliging like an obedient servant.

Sofia turned her head to kiss me on the neck, while her hand slowly went further down towards the top of my jeans. I was completely turned on now, with Sofia's right hand moving around the sensitive spot on my jeans in circles, her left hand playing with my neck.

Ever so slowly, her fingers moved towards the zip of my jeans, pulling the zip down. Before I knew it, Sofia's hand was inside my jeans. I almost gasped with surprise as soon as Sofia's hand went inside, but I somehow controlled myself to ensure nobody around would get suspicious.

Sofia knew her way around me pretty well, her hand playing with my organ. I had to grip the couch tightly to prevent my body from going out of control. But Sofia showed no mercy, moving her hand up and down with the perfect speed and force.

While the audience was busy watching the movie, I was having the greatest orgasm I've ever had.

Sofia gradually started moving her hand up and down with higher speed and force, forcing me to grab the couch even harder. It was all I could do to stifle my gasp as I reached the climax, my mind wild with pleasure.

Sofia gently relaxed her grip, and took out a few tissues from her purse to wipe her hands. I was completely zoned out, with no idea of my surroundings. My mind was in a different world altogether, and it took me some time to come back to my senses.

I saw Sofia smiling fondly at me, and I brought her closer to me to kiss her. She kissed me back, cuddling against my chest.

We had already missed half of the movie, and we did not really care about the movie anyway. We spent the rest of the movie just cuddling with each other, two hearts beating as one, enjoying our last few moments together.

28

I got busy with my studies in India. Around a week had passed since I had returned, but I had left my heart in Europe. While I was glad to reunite with my family and my friends, I felt incomplete without Sofia.

I was in my final year and had to write a thesis. Unlike my internship at Switzerland, I could not take the thesis lightly. My entire career depended on the thesis. I had worked hard to clear JEE, and to get good grades in my studies at IIT Kanpur. This thesis was the final hurdle that I had to ace before I could graduate with a successful degree. So I worked as hard as I could.

I was in constant touch with Sofia all along. She was preparing for her internship at Tel Aviv, and had to leave Germany in a week's time. We would do Skype calls at least once every two days.

Sofia was very excited for her internship in Israel, and I was happy for her. She was spending the time that she had before her internship to read up about the various techniques used in film production. She would get some training during her internship as well, but she wanted to study the concepts beforehand so that she could really hit the ground running during her internship. I couldn't help but smile at the thought that Sofia was so hardworking and ambitious, just like me.

I was also in constant touch with Laura. She had started her thesis after going back to her home university, and was doing well. She kept travelling to cities across Europe that had any sort of connection with Mozart, to gather research material for her thesis. She seemed happy.

My thesis was also going well, and my thesis guide was very happy with me. I expected to finish the thesis by the end of that semester. Considering my excellent grades and my research credentials (Hamza and Onur had given me great reviews), there were high chances that I could get into a good Master's program in US or Europe.

This was my seventh semester, and we had the placement season coming up. After the end of the semester, we had a one-month break, during which the placement interviews were expected to happen.

Most of my batch-mates were busy preparing for the placements. The top companies from every field, be it core or non-core, were expected to hire huge numbers from the campus. My computer science batch-mates were busy preparing for dream companies such as Facebook and Google. Those who were not interested in core profiles were preparing hard for non-core profiles related to management consulting, finance and marketing.

The environment was one of immense stress. Everyone was busy juggling multiple balls at the same time – courses, thesis and placement preparation. The placement cell was being considered holy, and the members of the placement cell were being worshipped during this period. After all, everyone wanted a good job right after campus.

I, however, had no interest in the campus placements. I was clear about my interest in research, and my credentials supported my interest. My professors thought that I wanted to undertake a career in research to pursue my passion in the field of computer science. Well, that was not really true, because I was not even half as passionate about computer science as my other batch-mates were.

My primary reason for wanting to pursue a career in research was that it was a guaranteed way to ensure that I would get the opportunity to stay in a good place of my choice abroad, either in US or Europe. Sofia would have found it very difficult to settle down in India, and I wanted to ensure I had the flexibility to settle down wherever I wanted. A good researcher could, to a large extent, choose the university where he wanted to teach.

Considering that I did not want to pursue a job directly after campus, I had been thinking about giving the placement interviews a miss and try for another research internship for the one month period.

I had been primarily looking for research projects in India because it would be very difficult to get a project abroad for just a month. However, it struck me one day while browsing through the universities – there was no harm in also trying for research projects in Tel Aviv!

Israel was not a very popular place to apply for research projects, so they might not be getting as many applications. As a result, there could be some possibility that they need someone for that duration. I could definitely try my luck. Sofia would be in Tel Aviv at that time, so it would be the perfect opportunity to meet her again and spend more time with her.

The best way to look for such internships was to search for universities in that area, look up the profiles of the professors in the computer science department, and send them an email requesting for a research project opportunity. The email needed to be customized according to the profile of the professor, to ensure that it would not be considered spam. If the professor needed someone for a research project, and he or she liked your profile, then there was a chance that you could be accepted for the internship.

So along with the professors in the leading engineering universities in India (which mainly consisted of the various IITs), I also started sending emails to professors in Israel. While I concentrated on the Tel Aviv University in Israel, I also sent emails to a few universities in other cities around Tel Aviv, to strengthen my chances.

The professors generally took a long time to reply to such emails, considering they received so many emails from all over the world requesting for internships. My situation, however, was different because of two reasons – First, this period was off-season for internships since students generally applied for internships during the summers. And second, I had applied to a country which was not as popular among students for research internships. As a result, I started receiving replies within a week's time.

As expected, most of the replies that I received were negative. I didn't lose hope and sent reminder emails to the professors who had not replied so far.

By then, Sofia had reached Tel Aviv and had started her training sessions. She was working hard during the training sessions, so our Skype calls had become less frequent now. However, she kept sending me text messages about how everything was going, and how much she was loving Tel Aviv. She mentioned that there was a lot to learn, and she was putting in extra hours to catch up with the others around her who were from a film production background.

Sofia had rented a flat in Tel Aviv with an Italian flatmate, Daniela. Daniela was a Master's student studying physics at the Tel Aviv University. She had just started her Master's, so she was also new to Tel Aviv. Sofia and Daniela had struck an instant chord, and had already become very close friends.

I kept receiving negative replies from most of the professors I had requested for an internship in India and Israel. I had almost begun to accept my fate and was about to start preparing for the placement season with my other batch-mates, when I received an unexpected reply from one of the professors at the Tel Aviv University which gave me a ray of hope.

The professor, named Amir Shadab, apologized for the late reply, saying he had been out of the country for the past few weeks and had just seen my email.

Amir worked in the area of cloud computing, and needed some help with one of the research projects that he was currently pursuing. My coding skills, along with my EPFL experience in cloud computing, seemed perfect for the role.

However, he would not be able to pay me much, due to lack of funds. He could only fund my flights and accommodation.

This opportunity seemed perfect for me. I had been paid really well during my internship at EPFL, and I still had some money left. That would be enough to fund this internship in Israel. After all, I would only need to worry about food and maybe some travelling expenses here and there. Considering Sofia would be in Tel Aviv and would be busy with her internship, I didn't foresee any major travelling plans.

I enthusiastically agreed for the project. This professor had emerged like a blessing, just when I had been about to lose all hope. And I was not going to let this opportunity go.

I couldn't wait to inform Sofia. I texted her, saying I had some good news for our next Skype call. I knew Sofia would not be able to withstand the curiosity. As expected, she called me within a minute. I told her how I had applied for internships in Israel. On hearing about the development with Amir, Sofia shrieked with delight.

"You're not kidding, right? You are actually coming to Tel Aviv? This is so awesome! We will have so much fun together. Oh my god, I love you so much," Sofia said, her words nearly incoherent due to her high-pitched excited voice.

I couldn't stop myself from laughing at her excitement. I was equally excited, and couldn't wait to meet Sofia again. I had applied to Israel only to test my luck; I couldn't believe I had actually got selected.

I had sent an acceptance email to Amir, thanking him for the opportunity. However, there was still a difficult step left – convincing my parents. They had a really tough time understanding why I would want to do another project so soon, and that too in Israel, of all places. They had not heard of anyone going to Israel for research. Frankly, I had also not heard of anyone going to Israel for research in computer science, but I couldn't say that. I also couldn't tell my parents the real reason why I wanted to go to Israel. They did not know about Sofia, and I didn't want to tell them yet as I wasn't sure how they would react, being slightly conservative.

So I told my parents that the Tel Aviv University is specifically well-known for the field of cloud computing, and Amir was a well-known professor in the field.

My parents trusted me. Even though they could not understand why I felt this internship was so important for my career, they reluctantly agreed to let me go to Israel. But only after multiple rounds of persuasion.

Excited, I started preparing all the required documents and also contacted a travel agent to initiate my visa process.

Everything was going really well, better than I could have ever planned. Sofia and I were very happy. We would get the chance to spend a month together soon. Sofia had already told me in a decisive tone that I would be staying with her.

"But won't Daniela have issues with me living in the same flat?" I asked Sofia. After all, I don't think I would have been very comfortable if I had a flatmate whose girlfriend had just moved in to live with him. It could be awkward for Daniela, I thought.

"Oh no, not at all. Daniela is a cool girl. I'll talk to her. She'll be okay. Oh Raj! I can't wait for us to live together!" Sofia said, her excitement showing in her voice.

The more I thought about it, the more I liked Sofia's idea. That way, I could try to convince Amir to let go of the accommodation allowance that he had promised me, but pay me an equivalent amount as stipend instead. And the best part – I would get to live with Sofia! I decided to speak to Amir about it closer to my departure date.

Everything was going perfect. A little too perfect, it seemed. And when something is going so perfect, things are bound to backfire.

Things did backfire, and in a way that neither of us could have ever predicted. In a way that nobody in the entire world had foreseen.

In July 2014, Israel bombed its neighbouring country Gaza, and Gaza replied with rocket attacks on Israel. This sequence of events was the start of a war which would go on to last for weeks, resulting in heavy loss of life and property on both sides. A war that would become known all over the world as the "2014 Israel-Gaza conflict", and would go down in history as one of the worst wars between any two countries.

A war that would go on to completely alter the life of an IITian nerd in a country more than four thousand kilometres away from the conflict.

29

While my batch-mates were focusing on the placements, I spent all my free time reading about the Israel-Gaza conflict. I subscribed to global magazines like the *Economist*, which covered articles related to the conflict in detail. I also scanned the newspapers every single day for more news about the conflict. In no time, I had become an expert on the topic, probably knowing more about the Israel-Gaza conflict than even the citizens of those countries.

Gaza was under the rule of a militant Islamic Palestinian organization named Hamas. The organization was regarded as a terrorist organization all over the world because of its militant roots and dictatorship rule.

In July 2014, some of the Hamas members had kidnapped and murdered three Israeli teenagers. The Israeli government had retaliated through a covert operation by bombing a few Hamas populated areas and arresting some Hamas militant leaders. The Hamas government had retaliated back by firing rockets into Israel, thus formally initiating the war.

The Israeli embassy in India had placed all visa applications on hold for the time being, until the situation improved in Israel. Considering that nobody knew when the situation would improve, my application was on hold for an indefinite period. I intimated the news to Amir, who said he completely understood the situation and would keep the internship position open for a few more weeks in case the situation in Israel improved and my visa application went through.

I was extremely worried about Sofia. Her film production company had disbanded the project on the traditions and culture of Israel, and had instead started covering the conditions of the Tel Aviv citizens affected by the war.

I had requested Sofia multiple times to get out of Israel and go back to Germany, but she did not listen to me. She felt this project was really important for her career, and did not want to abandon such a lucrative opportunity. I tried all means to plead and reason with her, but without any success. I sometimes cursed Sofia for being so ambitious. She was a determined woman and didn't get scared easily.

According to her, the war was not expected to last long. The Israeli citizens were optimistic about the war ending in a few days, considering that Israel was much stronger than Gaza. And Sofia, staying at Tel Aviv, naturally reflected that optimism.

I, however, was not so sure about the situation improving anytime soon. Especially from all the articles I read in the newspapers every single day, since I followed the conflict as closely as possible.

The situation actually was worse in Gaza compared to Israel, if we looked at the number of casualties. Israel, being a much more powerful country compared to Gaza, had better military intelligence and more advanced missile technologies. Combined with an advanced defence system, Israel was able to target

Hamas locations with better accuracy, while at the same time preventing the air attacks through their military intelligence.

It was a no-brainer that Israel would win the war. However, there were further casualties expected on both sides, and I only cared about one person who was caught in all this mess.

Sofia did nothing to ease my anxiety. Rather, my stress increased every time I talked to her these days. Sofia mentioned that there were a few covert Palestinian supporters in Israel, who carried out secret operations and attacks in Israel every now and then.

She told me that alarms often went off in Tel Aviv indicating some type of unrest, be it an impending air strike or an attack by some Hamas supporter. Whenever that happened, everyone would rush and hide wherever they could. Sofia always hid beneath the nearest staircase. According to her, that was the safest place that she could find.

During one such incident, while hiding under a staircase, Sofia observed some shooting on the street outside. She took a video of the incident through her cell phone for her film production company, and also sent that video to me.

Even though the video was slightly blurred with a dark background, I could clearly hear multiple gunshots, followed by yelling and screams of people. The screams sent shivers down my spine. I could hear those sounds even in my dreams these days, with my biggest fear being one of the gunshots hitting an innocent girl hiding under a staircase.

A few weeks passed like this. Every day, my heart sent prayers for the situation to improve in Israel. Gradually, one day at a time, the situation started improving. The number of attacks started reducing from both sides, finally resulting in a complete week without any attack from either side.

The newspaper articles started becoming more optimistic, with some articles even calling this an end to the conflict. Some journalists claimed that according to their sources, Israel and Gaza were on the verge of calling off the war by negotiating a deal.

To brighten things further, I received an email from the Israeli embassy in India that my visa process had been resumed, and I would get my visa in a couple of weeks. I took all these developments as a sign that everything was soon going to be okay.

Sofia reverberated similar signs from Tel Aviv, her confident nature adding on to the optimism. There were still some precautions the citizens tried to take whenever roaming around Tel Aviv alone or late at night, but there had been no incidents recently.

Sofia was really excited when she heard that my visa process had been resumed. “Everything seems to have turned out well in the end,” Sofia said one day during our Skype chat.

My parents were very apprehensive about me going to Israel during this tense situation. I tried to explain to them that the situation had improved now, but they did not want to listen to me. As parents, they really cared about me, and wanted me to be safe. I understood their concern.

If this had been a normal situation, I would have cancelled the plan of going to Israel without even thinking twice about it. But this was not a normal situation, and I couldn’t mention that to my parents.

I tried to convince them by telling them about the importance of the project that I was going to do at Israel. I told them this was a rare opportunity and would be really useful for my career prospects. I had been really lucky to be accepted for the project. My parents were not very convinced, but reluctantly agreed. They trusted me and my judgment, and eventually gave in to my decision.

I received my visa in a couple of weeks, and booked my flight tickets. I would fly to Israel as soon as my vacation started, just after the end of my thesis. I couldn't wait to get united with Sofia again.

Life seemed normal again. The newspaper articles on the Israel-Gaza conflict started referring to the conflict in the past tense. As Sofia had said, everything seemed to be going well.

Until that one fateful day, when my world unexpectedly came crashing down, shattering everything in my life to bits and pieces.

30

It was Saturday night, and I was partying with my friends, celebrating the completion of my thesis. I had not just finished my thesis a couple of weeks earlier than the deadline, but had also received an excellent review from my guide. My friends had decided to use this as an opportunity to get crazy drunk tonight, and had bought a full week's worth of alcohol for one night. I was very happy that night. Not just because I was done with my thesis, but also because there were only two weeks left for my flight to Israel. Just two weeks left before I would meet my Sofia again.

We were partying at a friend's room. My head was completely dizzy with all the alcohol, so I did not notice my phone vibrating. Accidentally, and I would thank my destiny forever for this, I glanced at my phone to realize that Sofia was calling me. If I had missed this call, I would have cursed myself all my life.

"Hi Sweetie," I said, picking up the phone.

There was complete silence from the other end. I thought I could probably not hear anything because of the noise in the room, so I went out.

"Sofia, can you hear me?" I spoke on the phone.

I still didn't hear anything for a while, and was about to disconnect the phone when I heard a voice speak in a very soft tone.

"Raj..." the voice said, so softly that I thought my drunk brain was playing games with me. Somehow, I felt slightly uneasy hearing the voice. It did not sound like Sofia's usual cheerful tone. It sounded...sad! No, not sad. It sounded, and my heart skipped a beat on the thought, pained? Yes, Sofia sounded as if she was in pain!

"Sofia, are you there?" I said again, speaking louder this time.

Complete silence.

"Sofia, are you there? Can you hear me?" I repeated, getting anxious now. Still no answer.

I was getting really tensed now. I repeated her name several times on the phone, but there was still no answer. And then the phone disconnected.

I called Sofia back, and waited eagerly for her to pick up the phone, my heartbeat rising with each ring of the phone.

"Oh c'mon, Sofia! Pick it up," I muttered, my panic level reaching peak high.

Sofia still did not pick up the phone. I tried calling her multiple times, but there was no answer. I dropped her a text, asking her to call me back ASAP.

All the alcohol in my blood seemed to have dissolved by now. I was fully alert, filled with anxiety. Something had happened to Sofia. Something bad. I could sense it. And I did not know what to do.

I needed to contact someone who could reach Sofia... someone who lived in Tel Aviv, maybe. I tried to recall the names of Sofia's friends from her conversations with me. There had to be someone I could contact.

And then I remembered. Sofia's roommate, Daniela! Daniela would know if something had happened to Sofia. Even if she did not know, she would be able to find out.

I did not have Daniela's phone number, so I tried the next best option. I rushed to my room and took out my laptop. I opened Sofia's Facebook page, and searched for Daniela in the list of her friends.

The search resulted in four girls with that name. Damn! I did not know Daniela's full name.

I opened each profile one by one, hoping to see something related to Tel Aviv in one of the profiles. None of the profiles had Tel Aviv mentioned.

Frustrated, I decided to send a message to all the four profiles. The right Daniela would reach out to me, I hoped.

Hi Daniela. Are you Sofia's roommate at Tel Aviv? I am her boyfriend. I have been trying to contact Sofia, but she is unreachable. Do you know where she is, and if she is alright? Please call me as soon as possible. And sorry for the random message, if you are not the right Daniela, the message read. I also mentioned my phone number at the end of the message.

And then the toughest part began – the endless wait. Helplessly, I sat down and started waiting for someone to call me.

My friends were probably too drunk to have noticed that I had been gone for so long. I really hoped it would remain that way. I had absolutely no strength to deal with my friends at this moment.

I hated being in such a powerless position, but there was nothing else I could do! I contemplated calling Laura, but then thought against it. Apart from my intuition, there was nothing else to suggest that Sofia was in pain, and I did not want to raise unnecessary panic in case Sofia was actually okay.

Restless, I looked at my phone every few seconds. I also checked my Facebook every now and then for a reply from Daniela. There was no reply so far. Damn! For all I knew, none of them might be Sofia's roommate. The Daniela I was looking for might have an account under a different name on Facebook, or might not have an account at all.

I tried calling Sofia again, hoping against hope that she would answer, but nobody picked up the phone.

I almost threw my phone on the wall in frustration, stopping myself at the last moment when I realized that the phone was my only chance to connect with Sofia at that moment.

Not knowing what to do, I laid down on my bed, and started browsing through Sofia's photos on my phone. Gosh, I loved this girl so much.

"Please, oh please, let Sofia be alright," I muttered, trying to pray. I had never prayed much in my life, but that night I prayed for Sofia with all my heart. That night was the longest and the hardest night of my life – a night that would remain etched in my memory forever.

31

I woke up with a start, to find my phone ringing at full volume. It took me a couple of seconds to get back to my senses, before I suddenly remembered the incidents from last night. Sofia!

I must have fallen asleep while waiting for someone to call me with any news. The alcohol from last night must have finally taken its toll on me.

I groped around the bed to find my cell phone, and finally found it lying on the floor.

I picked up the phone to check the caller. It was an unknown number. My heart started beating louder when I observed the country code – +972. It was an Israeli SIM card.

"Oh, please let Sofia be alright," I muttered to myself, once again, picking up the phone.

"Hello," I spoke on the phone.

I did not hear any reply for a few seconds, so I thought the caller could probably not hear my voice. I brought my face closer to the speaker.

"Hello? Who's there? Sofia, is this you?" I asked. I could hear my own heart beating by now.

I could suddenly hear heavy sobs from the other side, giving way to loud crying. The voice did not sound like Sofia's. My heart was bursting with anxiety now.

"Who's this? Why are you crying?" I asked. I found myself shaking with fear and worry, and grabbed a chair to steady myself.

"Raj... this is Daniela..." the voice began, barely able to speak in between all the crying. "Oh Raj... Sofia... poor Sofia... Raj..."

I was shaking so hard by now that I was afraid the phone would fall from my hands.

"What happened to Sofia? Tell me, Daniela. Sofia is okay, right?"

I could still only hear loud crying from the other end. "Tell me Daniela. Sofia is okay, right? Tell me!" I heard myself shouting, tears welling up in my eyes.

"Oh Raj... Sofia... Sofia is dead... last night... gunshots..."

I found myself dropping down to the bed, the phone slipping from my hand and falling to the floor. No, this could not happen. This could not happen to Sofia. Sofia could not be dead. No, tell me this was just a nightmare. This had to be a nightmare. Sofia could not leave me. She could not leave me alone.

I had gone numb with shock, my entire body shaking. I sat silently on the bed for a long time, tears streaming down my eyes. I had lost all my senses, not being able to comprehend anything for a long while.

Shock gave way to disbelief. No, Daniela was wrong. She had to be. Sofia would never ever leave me. Daniela did not know anything about Sofia and me. We were so close...how could she leave me alone!

The disbelief slowly turned to anger. Anger at Sofia for staying back in Israel despite all my pleadings. Anger at myself for not being there to save Sofia.

Anger at the world for the injustice of it all.

My eyes were moist, but my heart was still in denial. I was not shouting or crying loudly. I just sat there at the edge of my bed for what seemed like hours, before my heart suddenly burst into a flood of emotions.

And once that happened, I gave in to my emotions. What followed was a wail that could be heard across the corridors. I was crying so much that tears came gushing out of my eyes. My vision was blinded, my throat parched. I just kept shouting and crying.

My batch-mates, on hearing the wailing noise, came to my room to check on me. Seeing me in such a state, they tried to console me, but I was inconsolable. All I could think of was the unfairness of it all. I cried with all my heart, until the time I had no tears left in my eyes.

I cried for Sofia, and the pain she must have felt. I cried for our lost future. I cried and cried, until I had exhausted all my energy.

Something changed inside me that day. As my friends would tell me later, that fateful day, they witnessed a mourning that sent shivers down their spine whenever they thought about it.

32

I had called Daniela back the next day, and asked her how Sofia had died. Daniela had taken me through the sequence of events leading to Sofia's death.

Sofia had gone to a bar in Tel Aviv on Saturday evening with a few friends to party. Tel Aviv had not seen any attack from Hamas supporters in weeks, and everything had been assumed to be back to normal. However, that day, two Hamas supporters had stormed into the bar and opened fire on everyone. Around two dozen people had died on the spot, with half a dozen people injured.

I closed my eyes and tried to prevent myself from imagining Sofia lying in a pool of blood. *Oh, Sofia!*

"Was it quick?" I asked Daniela. "Or did Sofia endure any torture before she...you know..." I still couldn't bring myself to use the word "died" with Sofia.

Daniela mentioned that nobody knew all the facts yet, and the investigation was still going on. According to the medical team and police who had reached the spot after the massacre, Sofia had died on the spot. The bullet had hit Sofia in the forehead, so it had to be quick.

I closed my eyes, tears streaming down my face. A bullet to the forehead! It was such a waste of life. It felt so cruel. How could fate take away a person who was so good and so full of life! Sofia had never harmed anyone in her life. She had always been kind and gentle to everyone. The unfairness of it all made me even sadder.

Days passed. I had lost all purpose in my life. I hardly ever left my hostel room. I did not have any energy left in me anymore. I was completely drained and exhausted. Whatever little energy I had would be spent crying.

All I could do the whole day was look at Sofia's photos and remember all the good memories that we had shared. And all the good memories we had planned to share in the future.

I knew Sofia wouldn't have liked to see me in such a state, so I tried to take care of myself as much as I could. But it was so damn hard to stop myself from crying whenever I thought about Sofia.

I wanted to go to Israel at that very moment, even if just to see Sofia one last time before her... funeral. A pain shot through my heart on thinking about the funeral. Sofia and I had been planning our lives together. Why did fate have to be so unfair? Half a dozen people had survived the attack. Why couldn't Sofia be among the survivors?

My visa dates, however, still did not allow me to go to Israel for the next two weeks. I had called up the embassy and spoken to the customer care if they could allow me to go to Israel earlier, but to no effect. It would take time to reapply for the visa, which meant there was no way I could reach Tel Aviv in time for the funeral.

Not knowing what to do, I had called up Laura. Being one of Sofia's closest friends, she deserved to know about the incident. I told her everything. Laura was utterly shocked, and we cried together for hours on the phone, reminiscing about all the memories we had shared with Sofia.

"Italians do not need a visa to travel to Israel," Laura suddenly said in a decisive tone. "Don't worry, Raj. I will book a flight to Tel Aviv today itself and take care of everything. I have her dad's contact details, so I'll inform him as well. Her family needs to know."

I was glad to see Laura take charge of the situation, because I still could not bring myself to gather enough strength for this. Laura was strong and sensible, much more than I was, and I could trust her.

The next few days went by in a blur. I hardly ever left my hostel room, crying or thinking about Sofia all the time. My batch-mates were concerned for me, especially after seeing my distressed condition. I did not have the energy to deal with anyone, though, and kept myself locked in my room most of the time. I just wanted to be left alone.

The semester was about to end, and my travel date to Israel was drawing closer. And so I started emptying my room and packing my bags. At least that gave me something to look forward to.

On the day of my departure, I wished my batch-mates all the best for their placements, and left for Israel. Seeing how worried my friends were, I assured them that I would be all right. They did not seem entirely convinced, but they knew that I did not ever listen to anybody anyway.

Once I reached Israel, I checked into a hotel room. As I checked in, I couldn't help but remember how Sofia and I had decided that I would stay with Sofia when I reached Israel. My heart throbbed with pain whenever I thought about all the plans Sofia and I had made together.

I still had five days to go before my internship started. While booking my flight a long time back, I had intentionally booked it earlier because I had wanted to spend some free time with Sofia. Now, I decided to use these few days before the internship to get to know more about Sofia's last days.

I had been in touch with Laura in the past few days. She had not just booked the next available flight to Tel Aviv, but had also taken care of everything after Sofia's death. She had informed Sofia's family. Her dad, utterly devastated, had reached Tel Aviv as well. While I had been holed up in my room, Laura and Sofia's dad had taken care of the arrangements needed for the funeral.

The funeral had been a solemn affair, according to Laura, with just Sofia's dad, her roommate and her colleagues from her film production company present. They had all talked about how gentle and kind Sofia had always been. She had been liked by everyone around her, and had left a void that could never be filled. I wished I could have attended the funeral as well, though I wasn't sure I would have been able to handle myself on seeing Sofia's body.

In a way, I was slightly glad I had been forced to miss the funeral. I would now always remember Sofia as the kind and lively girl, dancing through the obstacles of life to achieve her dreams, instead of a lifeless girl lying in a coffin.

I knew I would be grateful to Laura forever for taking care of everything so well. I had texted Laura as soon as I had arrived at Tel Aviv, and we decided to catch up that evening. She was still at Tel Aviv for a couple of days, before she had to go back to Italy to resume her studies.

Laura was the last thread connecting me with Sofia, and the only person who could understand my pain. In fact, she was the only person I knew with whom I could actually share my pain.

I reached the café to find Laura already waiting inside. She got up as soon as she saw me, came running towards me and hugged me, sobbing heavily. I hugged her back, my eyes welling up with tears as well.

As we sat down and ordered our coffees, I couldn't help observing how much Laura had changed in the past few days. She didn't look like her usual cheery self anymore. She had lost weight, and also had dark circles under her eyes now. She seemed… exhausted.

It must have been really heart-wrenching to take care of the untimely funeral arrangements of such a close friend, that too in a different country. My respect for Laura grew multi-fold.

Laura told me everything about the last few days. How she and Sofia's dad had procured the body from the Israeli police department and how they had organized the funeral. It had not been easy to get custody of Sofia's body, considering that the investigation was still ongoing. However, Sofia's dad had talked to the German embassy in Israel and pulled a few strings to expedite the process. I had wanted to meet Sofia's dad as well, but Laura told me he had left back for Germany right after the funeral.

"Did the investigations yield any results? Do we know who was behind the attack yet?" I asked Laura. I had been following the news closely the last few days, but I had not heard of the police making any arrests yet. All they knew so far was that it was an attack by Hamas supporters.

However, Gaza had declined to take responsibility for the attacks, saying the attack had not been planned by them. It appeared like some Hamas supporters, unhappy with the ongoing peace proceedings between the two countries, had decided to take matters in their own hands. They had failed in stopping the peace proceedings, but they had succeeded in taking away my Sofia from me, forever.

Laura's account matched with what the newspapers had been claiming. "I can't believe Sofia's killers are still out there," I said, anger building up inside me. "A bullet to the forehead," I added, clenching my fists angrily. "How could they shoot someone so easily? How could they take away the life of such a good and passionate person, for their own selfish goals?"

"Don't worry Raj. This attack has the attention of the entire world now. The killers will definitely be found and punished," Laura said, trying to soothe me.

The coffees had arrived. Both of us were silent for a while, sipping our coffee. Laura suddenly reached for her purse. "I have something for you, Raj," she said, pulling out a phone. I immediately recognized the phone. It was Sofia's phone.

"I thought you might want to keep this... as a memory," Laura said softly.

I looked at the phone, speechless. This phone contained the life of my Sofia. "I am not sure if I... if I should be the one to keep this phone," I said. "Wouldn't Sofia's family want the phone?" I added.

"Believe me, Raj, Sofia would have wanted you to keep it," Laura said, placing her hand over my hand.

"Sofia used to talk about you all the time, you know. She and I were in touch even after she had come to Tel Aviv. She would never get tired of telling me how much she loved you. She saw you as her soul-mate, and had started planning her entire life with you," Laura said. "Frankly, I had become bored of hearing your name so many times in all our conversations, but talking about you made Sofia really happy. She was very proud of your hard work and achievements, Raj," Laura added, smiling sadly while remembering her conversations with Sofia.

I was quiet, my eyes still brimming with tears. "Sofia was such an angel, you know. She meant everything to me. I could have done anything just to make her smile," I said, recalling all the instances when I had felt proud on having brought a smile on Sofia's face.

"You need to move on, Raj," Laura said, placing her hand on mine. "I can understand the pain that you are currently going through. I know it is not easy to move on. But I also know that Sofia would have wanted you to be happy. Believe me, Sofia would not have wanted to see you in this state."

"Well, I also never wanted to live without Sofia, but she did not care, did she?" I asked, crying again. "She left me anyway."

"You really think Sofia did not care about you, Raj? Well, you have no idea about the extent to which she loved you. Sofia did not die immediately, Raj. While the bullet had hit her in the forehead, she died a few minutes later. And do you know what she did during the last few minutes of her life?" Laura asked.

A pain started shooting through my heart. I knew the answer, but did not want to hear it. "No, please don't tell me," I whispered, more to myself than to Laura.

Laura didn't stop though. "She called you, Raj. We checked her call log. The last call from her phone is to you, a few seconds after the attack. The time of the call lies in the window after the attack and before the arrival of the police."

"She was found dead on the spot. We had initially thought she had died instantaneously. But the time of the call proves otherwise," Laura said, letting me take it all in, waiting for me to realize the essence of what she had just said.

It all came back to me, the pain increasing in my heart. Sofia's call on the night of the attack. "Raj...," she had said in a pained voice. I had sensed from her voice that something was wrong.

Sofia, in her last few seconds, had tried to call me. She knew she was going to die, and she probably wanted to hear my voice for the last time. She must have been in incredible pain, but still she had tried to call me. A shiver ran through my body as I realized what this meant. *The last word out of her mouth, just before dying, was my name!*

Laura held my hand, knowing what I was going through. "Sofia loved you till her very last breath, Raj, and would have given up anything to be with you. Sofia did not have a choice, Raj. None of us could have predicted what happened," Laura said. "But you do have a choice. You are young and ambitious. You can either waste away your life in misery, or you can spend the rest of your life living for yourself, as Sofia would have always wanted."

"I know, but it is so tough! My heart hurts every day. It feels like a spear has pierced my heart," I cried, letting go of the flood of tears that I had been trying to hold so far. Laura didn't say anything. She just held my hands as I cried my heart out.

"Laura, I need a favour," I said. "Would you please show me the place... the bar where Sofia died?" A lump formed in my throat when I said "died", but I really needed to get used to the word now.

"Of course, Raj. That is not a problem at all. We can go even now if you wish," Laura said. "They closed down the bar after the shooting, though, and nobody is allowed to go inside," Laura added.

I really wanted to visit the place where my Sofia had breathed her last, even if the place had been closed down. We decided to go directly from the café to the bar.

While Laura guided me to the bar, I couldn't help but think of how different today would have been if Sofia had been alive. I would have been spending time with Sofia right now, going on a romantic walk or watching a movie together, wrapped in each other's arms.

I could not help but think of all the alternate possibilities that could have taken place on the day that Sofia had died. Sofia could have stayed at home instead. Sofia could have decided to go to a different bar. The attackers could have chosen a different bar. There were just so many possibilities. Why did fate decide to take my Sofia away from me instead? What had Sofia and I done to deserve such pain?

Laura stopped walking, and I looked ahead to find an isolated building, barricaded from all sides. The building had not been touched after the attack, so the full extent of the massacre was visible. The glass windows of the building had been shattered from the attack. The wooden door had holes from the gunshots. The building looked dark and desolate, a sad reminiscence of a bar which once must have been lively and popular.

Laura did not speak anything, letting me absorb the sight in complete silence. I looked at Laura, not knowing how to thank her for everything she had done and was still doing for me. For Sofia. She just nodded, her eyes conveying that there was no need for any words. Laura could relate to my pain.

We stood there for a long time, just looking at the bar where my Sofia had breathed her last. All I could do was long for the future that could have been. A future with Sofia alive by my side, laughing in her usual merry tone.

A strong breeze started blowing, and I could sense Sofia's presence around me. I felt as if Sofia was watching me, showering her love on me and telling me that she was okay. I could feel us dancing one more time, with Sofia's head resting on my chest. I could feel her strawberry fragrance taking over my senses, the way it always did.

Sofia was trying to say something, but I could not hear her. I stopped, trying to understand what she was saying. "I am sorry, Raj. I have always loved you the most. Always. Will you stay happy for me? Will you live for me?" I could hear Sofia whispering to me in a tone that was very different from her usual merry tone.

Sofia was pleading with me, her eyes brimming with tears. Tears for our love. Tears for our lost future... Tears for bringing me to this state.

I could feel myself kissing Sofia one last time, my hands caressing her face, gently wiping away her tears.

"Oh Sofia! For you, always," I heard myself whispering softly, my words lost in the breeze, the strawberry fragrance gradually becoming weaker.